THE BUXOM BANDITS

E. C. HERBERT

For information contact: info@outlawspublishing.com
Cover Design by Outlaws Publishing LLC
Published by Outlaws Publishing LLC
July 2024
10987654321

Prologue

There's a new twist to the Old West stage robbery…WOMEN.

That's right. A band of women have gotten together to form the stage robbing gang, who would be known as the Buxom Bandits.

What started out as five good friends, but bored women, got together once a month to go on a shopping spree in San Francisco. Now they get together once a month to rob stagecoaches. Dressed in the flashy dresses of a prostitute, and sporting much make-up to cover their identity, these five known pillars of the community set about robbing stages so they could give the money to those in need.

Eleonore ran an orphanage and was on the verge of losing everything she had built, after her husband died.

Mary, who had gone to prison along with her two brothers and their uncle for holding up a stage years before, was considered the leader of the gang and was the sheriff's wife. She had taught them all how to ride and shoot. Now with their friend in financial trouble, they decided to put their skills into action.

A newspaper writer, Abe Butler, started writing stories about these women stage robbers, who he dubbed Guardian Angels over Buxom Bandits.

Almira, one of the bandits, contacted him after reading a story he had written for the local paper in the town where they pulled off their first robbery.

They had a secret meeting with Abe and told him why they robbed the stage. They said if he would write only good things about them and what they did with the money, they would contact him again and give him exclusives about the stage robberies.

After the shooting of a stage guard, U.S. Marshall Harry Finch was called in.

Come, ride with him now as he goes hot on the heels of THE BUXOM BANDITS

Chapter 1

Harry was devastated and distraught. Arriving home from his last assignment, he was met at the railroad station by several of his and Amanda's friends along with Reverend Miller, but no Amanda or AJ.

There were no smiles, laughter, hugs, nor kisses to be had on his return from his assignment. Only five friends whose looks told him something was terribly wrong. Turning towards the reverend, Harry gave him a questioning look.

"There was a fire two nights ago, Harry," the reverend began. "Because of the cold, no one was out and about. Maybe if someone had been, the fire might have been spotted in time, but no one was. Your place was found burned to the ground, the only thing left standing was the rock fireplace."

There were no tears shed by Harry that morning, just words.

"Where are their bodies?" Harry asked, his voice cracking.

"The casket is over at the church. AJ is in Amanda's casket, just the way he was found, in her arms."

"In her arms," repeated Harry.

"She might have been aware of the fire and gone to his room to get him. We're not sure of course, but they were found together. You not being here, Phil put them together. If you want separate caskets though, I'll arrange it," Reverend Miller told him.

"I'd like to go to the church now," said Harry, pulling his shoulders back and up straight, and clearing his voice.

"Of course, Harry," said the reverend.

Harry spent the rest of the day and that night in the church with his beloved wife, Amanda, and his son, AJ. Reverend Miller's wife, Crystal, brought him some coffee and a plate of food, but Harry didn't want food, He wanted his family.

Next morning, the coffin was laid in the ground at Mount Sunrise Cemetery.

Harry was surprised by the number of town folks who attended the funeral. But he shouldn't have been. Amanda was a friend to all. Opening their home on several occasions for this person or that person. And everyone liked Harry.

It made no difference to Amanda, all she saw was someone who needed help and living by the words in the Bible, she was the Good Samaritan.

Crystal, the reverend,s wife, had laid out some food at their home. After the funeral, all those who attended were invited to join them and partake of the dishes she had prepared.

Later that day, Harry, having ridden out to his place, was back in his railcar which would be his home now until he decided what he wanted to do.

He wasn't sure if he wanted to rebuild the homestead or to relocate to a different town.

Although he had friends here and would have plenty of support, he just wasn't sure he wanted to live in the memories that were built here.

Harry's last assignment had brought him to the town of Ogallala. He had really liked the town and the sheriff there. Plus, it had a railroad and telegraph lines, everything he needed for his job, and a new beginning for him.

"I think if the head office doesn't have any problem with me moving, I'm going to move on to Ogallala," he told Reverend Miller, who had dropped by Harry's home on wheels later that afternoon.

"I've already sent a telegram to Washington and now I'm just waiting for an answer."

"You know, Harry. You can always stay with Crystal and I. If you want to rebuild the homestead, it would be no trouble," he told Harry.

"Thank you for the offer, Reverend. It means a lot to me, but I'm going to move on to Ogallala, if the office okays the move, which I'm sure they will."

Harry's mind was clear now and he contemplated the move and set about clearing up loose ends in town.

Paying a visit to the cemetery, he told Amanda of his decision and felt her reassuring hand on his shoulder. As he was speaking to her, the overcast sky opened up and the bright golden rays of the sun basked his upturned face with its warmth.

"I knew it would be okay with you," he whispered up to the heavens. "I'll always love you and AJ no matter where I am," he said aloud, then left the cemetery with the approval from his beloved Amanda.

Returning to his railcar, Harry set about making a pot of coffee. He was just pouring his first cup when his telegraph key started with its dots and dashes.

As he jotted down the message, a smile came over his face as he wrote the words, "permission granted."

The message went on to say he had another assignment. 'Denver, Colorado' he jotted down.

A band of robbers were believed to be responsible for holding up the stagecoaches and getting away with the strongboxes containing coins and Federal Reserve Bank drafts. Local law officials had been unable to apprehend them so far. His assignment was to go to Denver and get together with Sheriff Joe Day for all other information.

Condolences were offered.

Having their permission, he sought to make the move to Ogallala. Harry now only had to make an arrangement with the railroad to have his two cars picked up by the next train headed west to Ogallala. He planned on stopping for a day or two, before moving on to Denver.

A quick message to Sheriff Will Caldron in Ogallala and all that was left was to be picked up by the next train, which would be later that evening and arriving in Ogallala in two days. A trip he remembered well, having just come back from there.

Looking in his trophy case, he saw the pair of dice he had taken off Deuce Morgan, which were the original dice that gave him his gambling name.

I wonder if they hanged Deuce yet, were his thoughts, remembering the assignment he had just completed.

As Harry readied his railcar for the trip to Denver, Robbie stopped by to pay his respects and to see if he needed anything.

"Yes, there is something you can do for me. Go to the bank and see if Mr. Grant can come over. I need to talk with him," Harry told him.

Harry had decided to stay around one more day to take care of all his business. He wouldn't be returning, but would stay in Ogallala once his new mission was completed. Harry fired up the potbellied wood stove. Soon, the aroma of boiling coffee filled the room.

Shortly after his first cup, a knock sounded on the door. Mr. Grant from the bank came in. Giving Harry his condolences, he asked what he could do for him.

"I'm leaving Shady Pines. I would like you to sell off the land. Keep the money I owe the bank, then wire the remainder to the First National Bank of Ogallala," Harry told him.

"You have to know, Harry, you have friends here who will help you rebuild your home. I can give you a loan to rebuild."

"I thank you for that, Mr. Grant, but I can't stay here, much less rebuild a home that was ours. You understand that."

"Yes I do, Harry. Just remember you are always welcome back here. I'll take care of your property and see to it whatever monies are due you will get wired to the bank in Ogallala."

Harry didn't think he would get much sleep that night, but was surprised when he opened his eyes. The sun was up and the streets were busy with activity.

Taking care of everything he needed to do, Harry visited with Reverend Miller and got his blessing. Next, he went to the livery stable and made arrangements to have Duke brought to the train station by seven o'clock, as the Union Pacific would be in at eight.

Meeting Robbie on the streets, Harry brought him into the mercantile store where he purchased ten cents worth of blue rock candy and handed the small paper bag to him. Before parting, he gave Robbie a piece of paper with a person's name written on it.

"Don't lose that name, Robbie. That's the person in the head office in Washington who will always know how to contact me. If the day comes you are serious about being a marshal, you contact him. Okay?"

"Okay, Harry," said Robbie, extending his hand to Harry, who grasped it in a strong handshake.

"I'll miss the stories, Harry," Robbie said as he walked away. "Thanks for the candy."

All business completed, Harry fired up the stove, put on water for coffee, sat down and re-read the message he had jotted down earlier.

From Sheriff Joe Day, he read again. Harry's memories were telling him his name was known.

"I wonder why he needs me? Before becoming a sheriff, he was probably the baddest bounty hunter in the whole Midwest," Harry said out loud.

Shrugging his shoulders, he said to the four walls of the railcar, "Guess I'll have to wait to ask him face to face."

At seven o'clock, Duke was brought to the railcar where Harry hitched him into his stall and made sure he had water and added some oats into his feed bucket.

Harry was finishing up when the shrill whistle from the locomotive sounded its arrival. Harry, along with two workers from the railroad, hitched up the two railcars.

Everything was ready. Thirty minutes later, the locomotive's shrill whistle sounded its departure from the station.

As the train picked up speed, Harry was again aware of the constant rumble of the train and the swaying motion of his railcar, just like an old friend.

Not having much sleep, Harry soon felt his eyelids getting heavy as sleep beckoned. For the first time in two days, he was able to put everything that had happened together, and the reality of losing his wife and son sank in. The reality of never seeing them alive again became real. But as sleep overtook him, he was again in the presence of his beloved Amanda bouncing his little AJ's laughing figure on his knee.

The train ride was as Harry had remembered, long.

At one of the train stops, Harry made telegraph connection and sent a message to Sheriff Will in Ogallala saying he was stopping by on his way to Denver.

Will was at the train station waiting for his arrival.

"Harry, what a surprise seeing you back here so soon. I thought you were going to take some time to spend with your wife and son," Will said shaking Harry's hand.

"Amanda and AJ were lost in a fire, while I was gone," he told Will, his voice low and shaky as he told Will about the fire.

"Harry, I'm so sorry to hear that. If there is anything I can do for you, all you need to do is ask," Will told Harry.

"There is one thing you can do for me, now that you've asked," said Harry. "I need a place to stay."

"Why you are welcome to stay with me, Harry," Will told him.

"I mean I need a place to stay. I'm moving to Ogallala," he told Will.

"As you know, I'm on my way to Denver on assignment. When I return I'd like to have a place to move into. Do you suppose you can find me a place?" Harry asked.

"Just your luck, Harry. I know of a nice ranch about two miles out of town that's up for sale. I'll find out what the selling price is," he told Harry.

"Thanks Will, I appreciate anything you can find out for me."

The train's whistle told them the train was about to leave. Stepping from Harry's railcar, Will bid him farewell and to be safe.

Turning back to face Harry, "They hanged that fella Deuce you brought in," he said, as the train was pulling away from the station.

That's good, thought Harry smiling to himself hearing that news. *Virgil must be a happy person.*

Finally, after a long ride and several stops, the train's whistle signaled its arrival into Denver. And a bullet that almost ended his career.

Chapter 2

The day of Harry's arrival into Denver was bright, but not as hot for this time of the year as Harry thought it would be.

Sheriff Joe Day was waiting for Harry, when the Union Pacific's whistle signaled its arrival into the Denver station. He had received a telegram advising him of Harry's arrival time.

Sheriff Joe, as he was known by most of the townsfolk, was a no-nonsense sheriff. Standing six foot tall and weighing one-eighty five, this bushy faced lawman, wearing twin Colts tied low, was an ex-bounty hunter, gambler, soldier, and freight hauler.

He had driven a Schuttler Wagon in Colorado Charlie Utter's wagon train, loaded with seven prostitutes traveling from Denver to Deadwood in 1876.

It turned out, there were almost two hundred prostitutes on that wagon train. Deadwood was a gold boom town and was overrun with miners and prospectors seeking their share of the gold colored dirt, and with that came cards, whiskey, and women.

It was on this trip to Deadwood that Joe met J. B. Hickok who was better known as Wild Bill Hickok.

In the past, Wild Bill Hickok was a US Deputy Marshal, gambler, lawman and wagon driver. He was an intriguing figure and Joe spent many an evening sitting around the campfire listening to his tales that became even more colorful after Calamity Jane joined the train.

When Joe returned to Denver, he told his wife, Mary, all the tales he heard. But more important, he wanted to become a lawman and get out of the freight hauling business.

It took almost seven years, but Joe finally became a deputy to Sheriff Dan Morgan. Later on in a close election, which he won, he became Denver's sheriff.

Now after several stage robberies, which included federal funds and the shooting of an ex-lawman from his city, he received a message from the US Marshals Office in Washington advising him they were sending US Marshal Harry Finch to Denver to oversee this matter and he was to give the marshal his utmost cooperation.

When Sheriff Joe received the message, he was right at the point of contacting them himself. There had been a number of stage robberies lately in which large sums of money were taken from local businesses, both going in and out of the city. The town's people demanded Sheriff Joe do something more than he was doing to apprehend the robbers.

Sheriff Joe didn't know what they expected him to do. After all, the stage robberies hadn't actually taken place in Denver, but the surrounding areas and states.

Everyone on these stages said the robbers were women. There were three of them and they dressed in colorful clothes, wore lots of make-up, and were sexy as all git-out.

The local newspaper had named them the Buxom Bandits, having been described as full figured women by those they had robbed.

They were also believed to be prostitutes. This stemming from the colorful names they used, both for themselves and for the men folk on the stages.

Names such as Precious, Sunny, Sugar Daddy, Handsome, Honey and such.

One of the women had a travois strapped to her horse. This two pole, Indian drag sled would be found along with the empty strongbox after every robbery.

All the robberies were done in the same manor. They would be waiting around a bend in the road with six guns drawn and pointed at the stage driver.

They would demand the strongbox be tossed down where two women would dismount and strap it to the travois. One woman would demand that the passengers get out of the stage and hand over their wallets and, in some cases, their money belts. Once done, they would then cut the team loose, get back on their mounts, and hightail it out of there.

Sheriff Joe shared everything about the stage robberies with Harry.

"How many stages have been robbed?" asked Harry.

Has anyone ever been injured?" he asked.

"Only one flesh wound and it was Matt Davis. I had deputized Matt and sent him to Omaha to act as a guard on one of the larger shipments of money. We can talk to him whenever you like."

Joe told him and at the same time answered his other question.

"Seven robberies, Harry, and now the town's people are demanding these robberies stop, the bandits captured, and money replaced or they will fire me. Heck Harry, I have no authority anywhere but Denver," he continued.

Sheriff Joe was mistaken on the number of robberies that had taken place. For right at that moment just outside of Cheyenne, Wyoming in the area known as Deadman's Bend, three women on horseback with guns at the ready were standing in the middle of the road, waiting for the Overland Stage to make its appearance.

Sheriff Joe, along with the whole town of Denver, would be shocked if they knew who the Buxom Bandits were. The assumption they were prostitutes, based on the way they spoke and dressed, couldn't have been further from who they were like the light of the day was different from the dark of the night.

Sitting high and tall in the saddle, having shed her personal clothes for those of a soiled dove, was the ring leader Mary Day, the sheriff's wife.

Mary didn't fit the mold of a Midwestern woman, simply because she was born and raised in a northeastern town along with two brothers, who taught her how to ride and shoot a six gun. She was also as good with a Winchester, as most men she met. Mary would be considered tall amongst the other four, being almost six foot.

Her coal black hair was now styled into a bun which was hidden under an oversized cowboy hat pulled down low to conceal it. Mary's dime sized blueberry colored eyes, for which she was known, was typical of women in the midwest. This was a good thing because there was no way to disguise them.

Mary had come west to Denver after being released from jail where she served three years of a five year prison sentence for stage robbery. Ever since she could remember, she liked to steal stuff, even if it was of little value.

The day she caught her two brothers in the hay mow eating candy they had stolen from Aunt Tillie's Mercantile was the start of her career as a thief.

Along with her two brothers they would plan out what to steal and from whom. The three knew a lot about firearms, having a father and uncle who hunted just about year round. They were never lacking for some kind of meat with most meals.

After the death of their mother to the fever, their Uncle Lester moved in with them. Having just been released from prison for armed robbery, he had no other place to live. Within the month, he taught all three children how to shoot both a six gun and a rifle.

When times got rough, Uncle Lester would disappear for a week or so. When he returned, there would be enough money so the family could survive. Having listened to their uncle's stories, and being the age they were, it was pretty obvious he was up to his old occupation of a highway robber, once again.

That winter the death of their father changed their young lives forever, especially Mary's. Having no other way to support their home, the two boys joined their uncle in robbing travelers. These robbers were known as Highway Men.

They would leave Mary at home, while they traveled into the next county and robbed travelers until they had enough dollars to live on for a month or so.

While they were gone, Mary busied herself doing chores and teaching herself how to read, write, and count. That way, she could keep track of the money that was brought into the home.

During the course of the day, Mary would take her father's six gun, set up targets, and practice her shooting. Mary got to be good enough of a shot, she would join the men folk after Sunday morning church in a shooting contest, which she usually won. Prizes were usually animals such as a pig or a chicken, and later on the prize was a turkey. So these Sunday morning shooting contests became known as Turkey Shoots. Thanks to Mary, the Sinclair homestead was never lacking in fresh turkey meat.

As Mary got older, she longed to join her uncle and two brothers on one of their trips. After each trip, they would gather around the fireplace. Her brothers would tell her stories of what they had done, the people whose paths crossed theirs, and how they relieved them of all their money. Mary would listen and long for the day she would be able to join them.

The day Mary was waiting for finally came on her sixteenth birthday. That day, Mary joined her brothers and uncle as they packed their trail bags, saddled up, and rode away.

Mary's life would be forever changed that day. It seemed like overnight she was formed into the shape of a woman. Gone were the days of running around shirtless in the sun with her brothers or skinny dipping in the creek. Overnight, her legs grew eight inches till she was taller than her brothers. Her dark brown hair now turned a coal black in color. By seventeen, Mary Sinclair was a grown woman in all aspects related to womanhood.

There wasn't anything she couldn't do that men folk did, and she could out shoot the lot of them.

It was Mary who suggested to her brothers and uncle that they should go for a bigger stake than some travelers.

"I heard tell there was going to be a large shipment of money coming into town on the Overland stage tomorrow. It was Mildred from the bank who I overheard it from just yesterday, while we were in town," Mary told them.

"We can't rob a stage, can we Uncle Lester?" asked the younger brother Jessie.

"Never gave much thought to that one. But I don't see why we couldn't," Lester replied.

Hearing their Uncle Lester's answer, all three Sinclair kids said together, "Let's go for it, Uncle."

All they needed to do was find a good spot where they could easily hold the stage up and then simply wait for it to arrive.

That night, sitting around the campfire was one of excitement on Mary's part. They had just finished talking about the possibility of needing to shoot someone.

"If we get the draw on them quick enough, they won't have time to react. But if we don't, then there is a good possibility we will be shot at and have to return the gunfire."

Just this thought sent excited chills through Mary's body and her hand went down to grasp the butt of her Colt strapped around her waist.

The power to take someones life is in my hand, she thought.

Not knowing the time, the stage would pass through, the three rose early and hit the trail in search of a good place to hold up the stage.

Coming across a narrow place in the road, Lester surmised the stage would be traveling very slowly at that point, so they made plans to hold it up there.

The plans were Uncle Lester would pop out in front of the horses stopping them. Mary and her brothers would then pop out on either side of the stage with pistols drawn, pointing at the driver and inside the stage at any passengers. Orders would then be given for them to toss down their guns and the strongbox.

Knowing that firearms had value, they would collect both their weapons and the strongbox, and of course, their wallets.

The passengers would be ordered to step out and empty their pockets also. The success of this stage robbery netted them almost fifteen thousand dollars. This was more money than they had ever seen before, but it also netted them a price on their heads.

Chapter 3

There was much whooping and hollering once the strongbox was opened and it was revealed how much money was in it. As Lester watched, he knew from here on out, the children's lives would be forever changed, just as his had been years earlier when he had chosen this same path.

It was one thing holding up a passing trail rider and netting a few dollars It was another holding up a stage and stealing hundreds of thousands of dollars that was someone else's money.

"Let's get this money put away and get back to the homestead. We have a lot to talk about. But first, there are some places I need to stop at and some business needing tending to. We'll spend the night in Mosull," Uncle Lester finally told them.

Fifteen thousand dollars was more money than Lester had ever seen before. He had been sent to prison for armed robbery of a bank, but had only robbed it of four thousand dollars.

This was the payday he had been hoping for. Now it was here and with it, new issues to think about.

Lester wasn't wrong in his thinking. He had recognized the fella riding shotgun on the stage as one of the regular Saturday night card players down at Toby's Saloon.

There is no way he could have recognized me, were Lester's thoughts as they rode.

Turns out, Lester was wrong.

"I'm sure that was Lester Sinclair," Oscar, who was riding shotgun, told Leo Benson who drove the stage that day.

"How do you know that," Leo asked? "They were all wearing masks."

"I recognized his saddle," he told him.

"His saddle!" exclaimed Leo.

"His saddle. There was some beautiful tooling work done to it, along with the saddle horn being in the shape of a horse's head. I accepted that saddle when Lester couldn't pay up in a card game bet. Later on when he had some money, I sold it back to him. I'd recognize it anywhere," Oscar told him.

"He lives about three miles out of town on Jack Sinclair's place. He's Jack's brother who moved in right after the mother passed."

"We need to get to the sheriff as soon as we make town. No one holds up my stage and gets away with it," Leo told Oscar.

Kelly Cartwright, the sheriff of Manchester Province sat and listened as Oscar described the saddle he recognized as belonging to Lester Sinclair and to the fact there were three others with him, one being a female, fit right in with it being the Sinclair children also.

Gathering a small posse together, Sheriff Cartwright headed out to the Sinclair homestead. Finding the place deserted, he had his men take their horses and together they hid out in the barn and waited, although he knew they should have beat the stage and were probably gone. But there was no way they could have known they were recognized, so he was hoping they would show up.

For Lester, the ride back to the homestead seemingly took forever. Having taken care of some business, they were finally headed home.

Mary was undergoing some terrible cramping and they had to stop several times to take a break and let her cramping subside enough to ride some more.

The smile on all their faces upon seeing their home was short lived, when they opened the barn door to put their horses away. There to greet them, with pistols drawn, were Sheriff Cartwright and his posse of three.

The day Mary had waited for when she could ride with her uncle and brothers was short lived.

Mary was tried along with her brothers and uncle. They each received a prison sentence of which she served three years before gaining her freedom early for good behavior. Her uncle had received the maximum sentence of twenty-five years along with her two brothers who had received ten years each.

Even now as she rode onto the old homestead alone, the excitement of that day years before put butterflies in her stomach and a smile on her face. Mary's plan was to get a job, sell off the homestead, and head out west to California, leaving messages for her brothers.

Being Sunday, and nothing in the house as far as food goes, Mary headed into town. She figured to go look up Reverend Jackson, who she thought wouldn't judge her and could lend a helping hand. It was still early enough that the Sunday Social would still be going on.

Sunday Social was in full swing, when Mary rode up to the church. She had changed into one of her old dresses and made herself up the best she could. As she approached the church social gathering, Reverend Jackson saw her and was already headed in her direction. He stopped to tap Lynnette Harris on the shoulder as a signal for her to follow. They walked together to meet Mary.

"Well, well, Miss Sinclair," was the reverend's warm welcome, which was echoed by Lynnette. Both extending their hands in welcoming her.

Mary was surprised by those words and took some comfort in them as she was introduced to those who were there. All of the women and most all the menfolk showed her warm welcomes.

Lynnette Harris and her husband owned and operated a local freight hauling business and was expanding it to offer a western route. They needed another person in the office to gather in business and to operate that western route.

Lynnette offered Mary that job if she wanted it. Mary couldn't believe her good luck. Here she was, fresh out of prison and being welcomed into the fold, even being offered a job.

"This is what we can pay you to start. You will also receive a percentage of any business you bring in," Lynnette offered.

Mary listened and a new excitement ran through her body. She just couldn't believe her new found luck.

"What do you say? Do you want the job," she asked?

"Oh yes, Lynnette," she answered. "But why are you doing this for me. You know who I am and what I did, don't you?"

"Yes Mary, we all know, but we also believe in second chances. Here's your second chance." Lynnette answered.

Mary noticed one guy who sat off by himself slowly picking at his food. He was handsome in his own way. His face had a single expression on it, which Mary would learn seldom changed. Tapping Lynnette on the arm, Mary asked who he was.

"Oh, that's Joe Day, he works for us as a driver," Lynnette answered.

Lynnette noticed a sparkle in Mary's eyes as she spoke. She asked Mary, "Do you want to meet him?"

Nodding her head, Lynnette led her over to where Joe sat. He looked up as they arrived at his table, then stood and removed his hat all gentleman like.

"Joe, this is Mary," she said introducing her. "And Mary, this is Joe Day."

Joe Day, Mary repeated in her mind. *Mary Sinclair Day. Ummm. Sounds good.* All this was going through Mary's mind at the speed of light.

Something in his looks told her, here was the man for her. They say when the right person comes into your life you would know it. Mary hadn't believed that till now.

Butterflies in her stomach spoke to her, *here was the man for you,* and she wasn't going to let this minute pass by so she extended her hand and gave him her delightful smile.

Leaving the two of them there, Lynnette turned to walk away. As she did, she looked back over her shoulder and said, "I'll see you tomorrow morning at eight o'clock. Joe will tell you where the office is."

It didn't take long for Mary to realize if you wanted to have a conversation with Joe, well, you needed to be the one doing the talking. Joe didn't know how to speak a five word sentence, if his life depended on it. So knowing that, Mary just started talking and asking questions that didn't need long answers.

There was something about Joe that captured her attention. Before long, the social started to break up, at which time Joe offered her a ride home in his wagon.

"Bill and Mildred Stanley is the only other ranch past my place," she told him.

"I bought their place last year. They moved to California," he told her.

Two things happened in Mary's life, the next day.

First, she took the job Lynnette offered her, and second, she started seeing Joe.

Stan Harris hired another team driver to take over Joe's route and Joe became their long haul driver, a job he loved and was suited for one-hundred percent.

Although a quiet man, Joe could handle himself quite well. He was basically a loner, except when he was with Mary. Soon Joe asked Mary to marry him and they were married. Mary sold the homestead and moved in with Joe. Mary's bubbly personality slowly changed to being more like Joe's.

Although Joe never said anything to Mary, if she started to get talkative, he would simply get up from his chair and walk from the room.

Soon, Mary had established a very lucrative western hauling route and Joe found himself on the road more than he wanted to be. He didn't mind being gone a couple of days at a time. But over a week, he was getting sick of it. He told Mary this, one night he was home after supper, while he and Mary sat on the seldom used porch swing, drinking coffee.

"What do you want to do?" she asked him.

To Mary's surprise, Joe started to talk. When he did, she saw the man she always knew was hiding inside. From that moment on, it no longer bothered her if he spoke much or not at all.

"I want us to move to Denver. We can start our own freight hauling business out there. It's a growing place, as you know by the orders you get for freight going there," he told her.

As Joe spoke, Mary listened. Soon, his voice took on some excitement, which brought back memories of her own.

"I even found us a place," he told her.

"What do you mean you found us a place? This is the first I'm hearing all this. What if I don't want to leave here?" she asked.

"The place is right on Main Street. It's a small storefront type building with living quarters above it. It will be perfect for us. And for a dollar a week, I can store a wagon and board two horses at the livery stable," he told her.

This is how Mary and Joe Day ended up in Denver.

Lynnette and Stan didn't want to see them leave. But Mary and Lynnette worked out some hauling arrangements, where she would get a percentage of any freight she could get them on the return journey from Denver.

Within the week and the wagon packed, Joe and Mary were on their way to Denver and a new life.

It didn't take long for Mary to get the business up and operating at a large profit. Plus, with the extra from the business she got for Lynnette, they were doing quite well.

Joe had sold off his place and they bought a small ranch just outside of Denver in Pine Gap. Then Joe, out of the clear blue sky, hit Mary with another surprise.

Returning home after driving a wagon to Deadwood, Joe informed her he wanted to become a lawman.

Being married to Joe for several years, Mary knew that once he made up his mind about something, there was no use trying to talk him out of it. If Joe wanted to be a lawman, he was already one in his mind.

The only thing Mary told him was, she wasn't moving. So if he wanted to be a lawman, it would have to be right here in Denver.

The times Joe wasn't hauling freight were spent with Sheriff Dan Morgan, learning everything he could about the law and what it was like wearing the badge.

All this time while Joe was with the sheriff, Mary was left alone more and more, but Joe was loving it and seemed happier than he had been in quite a while.

As for Mary, she became friends with several of the other businesswomen in Denver. There was Sara Davis, who owned the local bakery, along with her best friend Leila Johnson.

Looking at the two, they could easily be sisters. They had been friends all their lives, having been born and raised in Denver.

Almira Kincaid had moved to Denver with her businessman husband ten years ago and worked as a telegraph operator and ticket agent. She was a good friend of both Sarah and Leila.

And then there was Kitty, a blond bombshell who was the town's gossip and a widow.

Every Wednesday, the five would meet at Almira's ranch where they would cut loose, drink a little whiskey and listen to all the gossip Kitty had stored up all week.

Once a month, they would take the train to San Francisco for a weekend of shopping and fun.

It was on one of these weekend trips that Mary told them about her skills with a rifle and a pistol. She told them she missed shooting. The others told Mary they would love to learn to shoot and asked her to teach them.

When they were in San Francisco, they went to a gun store and purchased pistols and ammo. On the next Wednesday night, they hitched up a wagon and went out of town to find an area to practice in.

Mary couldn't believe how clumsy they were, those first couple of times out. But by the third week, they all started to improve.

Mary wasn't sure what all this was building up to, but it felt good to be shooting again. With every kabooooom, old memories came back to her and the desires she had felt at sixteen, surfaced.

Mary had written her Uncle Lester in prison a few times and heard back from him twice, then no more letters. With every letter she sent her brothers, she received letters back.

Both were well, but had added on prison time for bad behavior. Neither one had taken to prison life. So now, when they should be getting out, they found themselves with more time to serve.

From reading her brother's letters, it became apparent they were planning on looking her up, when they did get out. The thought, at the time, made her cringe.

Mary put these thoughts away.

I'll deal with them if and when the time comes, she told herself. *For now, they are still in prison.*

Chapter 4

The five women were getting bored when they met Eleonore Keeton.

Eleonore, a widow lady in her early fifties, had been left well-off by her late husband. Eleonore ran a home for orphaned children called the Guardian Angel. Not having a family, Eleonore started a home for orphaned children. This gave her a family and kept her busy. And as she would tell you, "young."

Along with the orphanage, Eleonore had started helping out several families who had fallen on some bad times. This she kept hidden from everyone. She would deliver food baskets and sometimes an envelope with money in it, when their rent or mortgage payment was due.

This added to her financial burden. Soon, she found herself in financial troubles and in danger of losing her ranch, which is where the orphanage is located.

The five women had met Eleonore several months earlier at a church social and had become instant friends, partly due to the fact their friend, Kitty, was also a widow. They all liked visiting her ranch for some playtime with the kids. Many times, they would bring small toys or some items of clothing the children needed.

It was on one of these visits they found Eleonore in tears, which she tried to hide before they noticed but she just couldn't.

"Eleonore, what's the matter?" asked Mary, as the five rushed to her side.

"Jim Keeton, the bank president, stopped by today. He told me the bank needed a payment on the mortgage for the ranch or the bank was going to have to foreclose on it and I will lose everything," she stated with a cracking voice.

Tears were flowing all the way around as Mary comforted Eleonore's head on her shoulder. It was at this very instant Mary knew exactly what she needed to do. She knew once she shared her idea with the others, they would go along with her plan.

Over coffee and cookies, Mary learned all about what extra Eleonore had been doing for those who needed assistance. How she had forgone paying her own mortgage to help these families out. As they left, telling Eleonore not to worry, the five headed back to town.

"Let's stop here for a minute girls," Mary said, as they came upon Bear Claw Creek.

Stepping down from their mounts, Mary started in.

"I know how we can help Eleonore," she stated.

"We're listening," all four said together and now waited to see what Mary had to say.

Throwing caution to the wind, Mary started to speak.

"Years ago, my brothers, my uncle, and myself, used to rob folks as they traveled the country side. As a matter of fact, that's how we made a living after our daddy died. We would ambush travelers, steal all their money and whatever other things they might carry of value," she told them.

Her friends stood in utter silence and amazement as she told her story. After telling them she had gone to jail for stage robbery, which really got their attention, she started to lay out a plan to help their friend Eleonore out of the financial mess she was in.

"We all know how to use a gun. We all can ride like the wind. If we wear disguises and are careful not to let on to anyone what we are doing, we can ambush travelers, relieve them of their money and leave it in a basket on Eleonore's front porch."

Hearing what Mary was saying intrigued them. It sounded like a good idea to help out their friend. So the next time when they went out of town and into the city, they purchased some female clothes that were more related to what a prostitute would wear. Next, they bought wigs and make-up. When they returned home, they went to Bear Claw Creek and found a good hiding place for their outfits.

It was Almira who asked, "How are we going to rob complete strangers and get away with it? As soon as your husband Joe hears there were five women, he will know right away that it was us."

"We won't all take part in the robbery. I figure between only two or three of us, while the others look on from a hiding place with rifles ready, in case they are needed," Mary told them.

Kitty's eyes traveled across the faces of the others, as the realization as to what could take place during the robbery sunk in.

As if she read their minds, Mary spoke.

"Yes," she said. "You'll have to be ready to shoot someone if you have to."

Mary finished with, "there's a good chance we could get shot also."

Eyebrows went up on all of their faces.

"Well we could!" Mary stated with a stern voice. "We don't know who we are stopping to rob. Some cowboy just might test us and pull out his gun. If that happens, we all have to be ready to shoot him before he can shoot one of us."

What the four thought as something being fun to do, now took on a completely different face.

"Shoot another person! I don't know if I could," Kitty exclaimed.

"Listen, if anyone of you thought this was going to be a game to play, you're mistaken. If you don't think you can shoot another person if need be, this isn't going to work. Whomever are the two who stages the robbery, needs to be assured that you will have their backs and will defend them from harm, even if it means shooting and possibly killing another person," Mary said.

"I'm in," Sarah said, breaking the silence.

"Me to," followed Leila.

"Let's do this," Almira said. "I'm in also."

"Don't think you're leaving me out," Kitty said, wearing a big smile. "I'm in."

On that day, the five women swore alliance to one another and would soon become known as the Buxom Bandits.

"Where are we going to ambush from?" asked Kitty.

"We need to decide on that," answered Mary.

"Well, I say we continue taking our monthly trip into San Francisco. Once there, we can lease horses from one of the livery stables, ride out of town, and find a good place to change and put on our make-up. Then ambush from there," said Sarah.

"Let's lease our horses from different places and not check into the same hotel at the same time," Kitty said, tossing in her two cents worth to the conversation.

Concerned voices from earlier, now were excited as they started to work out some of the details.

"There are lots of small towns we pass through just before we get to San Francisco. I would imagine because the train doesn't stop at them, there will be plenty of travelers on the road to the city. We have to scout it out and decide on a good place to stage our ambush," Mary told them.

A sudden burst of laughter from Kitty got everyone's attention.

"Whatever you're thinking, you need to be sharing with the rest of us," said Leila.

"I was thinking we ought to make our victims strip down to their undergarments," she told them. "Picture that!"

Laughter was heard from them all.

"Imagine, riding into the city in your undergarments, finding the sheriff and telling him you were robbed of your money and clothes by a couple of women who appeared to be whores. Then told to get out of here."

"Great idea," Mary said, joined by laughter from the group.

It was a good thing their weekend trip was for the upcoming weekend, because neither one of them did a very good job at hiding their excitement.

Joe, Mary's husband, had noticed a difference in her as the weekend approached. But he knew it was her weekend away with the girls, which was always exciting to her.

It was also a weekend Joe could spend with a couple of friends and not have to worry about the wife getting upset if he played cards, smoked a cigar, or sat on the riverbank and fished all day. Yup, the weekend was as important to him as it was to Mary. He just never let onto that fact.

Three o'clock Thursday afternoon, Mary, Sarah, Leila, Almira, and Kitty boarded the train for San Francisco for what would be the start of a new career for the five of them. They had decided, once in San Francisco they would make like strangers.

As soon as they stepped off the train, they would go their separate ways, not having any contact with each other until meeting up on the road out of the city.

It was decided that Mary would leave first. Then the others would follow at half hour intervals and just keep riding until they met up wherever Mary would have decided was the right place to do their first ambush.

The last town the train passed through before reaching San Francisco was Butterman Bluff, a small town about ten miles from the city.

The train went through a crossing where they spotted a couple of old abandoned shacks and a road sign reading 'San Francisco 4 miles.' They decided this would be the place they would meet up.

"That place will be a good spot to work out of. We can stay hidden there and then follow the traveler we want to rob," said Mary.

"Seems we are taking a big chance not knowing how much money a person is carrying," Almira told them.

"Do you have another idea to share with us?" asked Leila.

"As a matter of fact I do," Mary replied.

"We're all ears," said the others, wondering what she had in mind.

"I have all the stage schedules and freight hauling tariffs. I can tell you which coaches will be carrying a strongbox and which freight company will be hauling silver or gold. They give me the schedule, so I can inform my husband, the sheriff," Mary said.

"You don't think we should hold up the stage or one of the freight wagons, do you?" Sarah questioned.

"Sure I do. Why not?" Almira replied. "We could rob passing travelers and get a few dollars. But we would know in advance as to the sum of money we could get from robbing a stage or a freight wagon, not to mention any extra we might get from any passengers on the stage."

The looks that passed between the five of them said it all.

"We will become stage robbers extraordinaire," Mary piped in.

With that, they all started laughing.

"How do we rob a stage?" asked Sarah.

"We'll need to put up a road block, so the stage will come to a complete stop. It will take at least three of us to perform the actual robbery, but that will be determined by the number of passengers on the stage," Mary told them.

Looking to Almira, "Will you know how many passengers will be on a given stage?" Mary asked.

"I can," Almira told them. "I simply have to ask when I get a telegraph with the stage's time of arrival and what it was carrying."

"Where do the stages come in from?" asked Sarah, excitement still in her voice.

"There's a stage that comes in from Ogallala, and one that comes in from Salt Lake. The stage from Salt Lake usually always carries a strongbox and is usually filled up with passengers," Almira told them.

"Have there been any stage robberies that you know of?" asked Kitty.

"I can answer that. No, there hasn't been. At least not in a long time. Joe has never had a stage robbery to talk about or investigate since he has been sheriff," said Mary.

"That's good. Isn't it?" Kitty asked. "We will be a complete surprise. No one will be expecting a robbery, so there probably won't be any gunplay involved."

"You're probably right there," said Mary. "But we still need to be aware there could be. Then realize everything will change in our lives after we pull off our first robbery. There is no going back to the here and now. Although no one will know who we are, we can never go back to who we were. We will be wanted for armed robbery. If we should get caught, we will be looking at some serious jail time. You all understand that, don't you?"

Mary's voice had taken on a serious tone and she looked at each one of her friends.

"You all understand that, don't you?" she repeated.

They all nodded their heads that they understood what she was saying.

"We won't keep any of the monies robbed for ourselves," Mary told them. "It all goes to helping Eleonore."

Chapter 5

It would be a week before the five female friends would rob their first stage. In that time, Mary questioned her husband to get as much information about what lay between Denver and Salt Lake.

It might have been the name, or the fact it was only about a four hour horseback ride out of Denver, where Mary decided they would do their first stage robbery. A place called Buttercup Basin.

They would leave on the Thursday morning train, bound for their weekend trip to San Francisco. But would get off when it made a stop at Dawson's Landing.

At Dawson's Landing, two of the girls would buy their horses from one of the three livery stables. Two girls would purchase their saddles and horses from one of the other stables. Mary would purchase a horse and saddle from the remaining livery.

Buttercup Basin was two hours out from Dawson's Landing, heading in the direction of Denver.

Mary figured that they would hold up the stage. Then afterward, return to Dawson's Landing where they would sell back their horses and board the next train to San Francisco, figuring the robbed stage wouldn't come back to Dawson's Landing, but continue on to Denver.

"We will have to come up with something different next time as far as transportation goes. Hopefully the three of us can pull off the robbery, so that nothing will ever be mentioned concerning five women," Mary told the group.

In the meantime, Almira and Kitty practiced a small dance number they would perform, as an added feature to the robbery.

"Kick up a little dust, show a little leg, it will take the sting out of being robbed and having their clothes stolen. And it will play into the prostitution theme we want to portray," Kitty laughed.

The day they boarded the train for their weekend trip to San Francisco was a hot one. August in Denver could be like that.

Along with their usual luggage, they carried a separate bag which held their fancy whoring dresses and makeup, along with six guns and broken down rifles.

When they got off the train at Dawson's Landing, they left instructions for their luggage to go on to San Francisco where they would retrieve them later at the depot there.

Excitement filled the air, that morning, as they stood outside on the train platform, each telling their short story about not being able to "sleep a wink" last night due to their excitement.

Stories to which Mary added with a wink, "and neither did Joe."

Her statement drawing laughter from the others.

The far off whistle told them the train was arriving and it pulled into view shortly after the whistle was heard. Once the train was underway, Sarah, in a whispered but excited voice asked again.

"How much money was going to be in the strongbox?"

"For the thirteenth time, somewhere around seventeen thousand dollars," Almira repeated.

The girls still couldn't believe the amount of money they would have very shortly from now and how it was going to help out their dear friend Eleonore.

Seventeen thousand dollars would be more than enough to pay off Eleonore's mortgage with the bank. They also knew it would draw a lot of attention from the bank's president if Eleonore was to go in with that amount of money. So it was decided Sarah would set up a trust fund with The Bank of San Francisco in the name of Sarah Smiles. She would send from there a bank draft to the Denver National Bank and Trust for three months advance on Eleonore's mortgage.

They didn't know it at the time, but over the next several months, bank accounts would be opened in several different banks under several different names.

Cash money would appear on Eleonore's doorstep, so she could pay off all of her tabs in town with the different merchants.

The first envelope to appear on her doorstep advised her strongly not to divulge where she had gotten the money, except to say if asked, a rich relative had passed and had set up a trust fund in her name. And that's all she knew about that.

Arriving in Dawson's Landing four hours before the stage was due in, and six hours before its destiny with the Buxom Bandits at Buttercup Basin, Mary and the girls set about on their planned schedule. They were soon on the road.

Mary and Kitty arrived at Buttercup Basin first. Surveying the area, Mary found an excellent spot for two of the girls to hide and also a good spot to drag a fallen tree across the road to stop the stage, which was their intention.

Stop the stage, hold it up, get the strongbox and have any passengers get out and remove their clothes down to their under garments. Then take their wallets, watches, rings, and money belts. Whatever they had of value. Cut the team of horses loose, then get out of there and back to Dawson's Landing in enough time to catch the next train to San Francisco.

Each one of the girls had their own chore to perform, once the robbery was underway.

For their first robbery, Sarah and Leila would be the backup and stay hidden from everyone, but ready to shoot, if needed. Mary would give the orders and control the stage driver and his partner.

Kitty was to be in charge of any passengers that were on the stage and also to talk lovey dovey to any of the males in the best prostitute's voice she could muster. Along with Almira, the two would carouse around some with the passengers before relieving them of personal possessions and their clothes.

The strongbox would be tied to an Indian style travois and dragged from the robbery site.

Almira was a great horsewoman and chosen to be the one in charge of the strongbox. Right at this very moment, she couldn't believe what she was about to become a part of. Although for the first time in the past two years, her heart was racing with excitement. Gone were any thoughts in the negative as to what she was about to do alongside her four female friends.

And it wasn't just her that felt this way.

"Almira, give me a hand would ya," Mary's voice interrupted her thoughts.

Mary was off of her horse and was tying a rope around a big tree limb, so it could be dragged across the road in order to stop the stage.

As Almira dismounted, she saw Sarah and Leila moving some brush around next to a large rock so they had cover to hide behind, while they watched the robbery take place. Ever ready to lend a hand, if needed.

All three would stay on their horses until the strongbox was tossed down and the driver and his partner were on the ground, along with all passengers.

Almira and Kitty would then put on their little show, while relieving them of their personal property. After that was done, they would then have everyone take off their boots, which were to be tossed away, and strip down to their undergarments.

Their clothes were to be stuffed into a grain sack and Mary would take off with them and leave them on the road ahead.

Mary decided not to cut the team loose, she wanted the girls to be able to get underway as quickly as possible, so they could circle back to Dawson's Landing.

Having dragged the tree limb into place across the road, all five started taking off their own clothes and putting on the fancy whore dresses.

Although all five were pretty well endowed, they no less stuffed the fancy brassieres to the max enhancing their forms. Makeup was smeared on in excess, especially the red lipstick and eye shadow. Once this was done, the girls had to admit it would be quite difficult to recognize them.

Now, the wait.

Mary and the others didn't have anything to worry about on this their first stage robbery.

Everything went off like clockwork. Soon, all five were on the train to San Francisco, each feeling more alive than they had in months, and in some cases years. Plus, they were thousands of dollars richer than when they started out.

In San Francisco, Sarah set up a trust fund as planned with Eleonore as beneficiary, so she could transfer funds from it.

For now, Mary and the girls were happy and they didn't mention the stage robbery at all between them. But things happened on their return trip home that got Mary to thinking they might just be of service to others.

On the train from San Francisco, the five befriended a young woman of nineteen years.

Black eyed and bloodied, cracked lips, they learned she had answered an ad in her local paper for young attractive girls wishing a future as dancers, singers, and bar girls in the booming city of San Francisco. Only to arrive without money, forced into prostitution and sexual slavery by a cruel madam who had a couple of enforcers who kept her girls in line through beatings, and even rape.

This young girl, whose name was Pearl Bailey, had purchased a train ticket for as far away as she could get and had escaped her madam, after this last beating.

Mary had a thought about Eleonore and maybe she might want to expand her ranch to take in girls such as Pearl, provided there were enough monies to do so.

The second thing that captured Mary's attention was the story she read in the *Dawson's Landing Gazette*, once they arrived there.

On the very front page in big block letters were the words, THE BUXOM BANDITS STRIKE! Hell, they had already been tagged with a title.

Mary read the story before telling the others. She found whoever had written it, injected some humor so it enlightened the whole robbery, especially the part about having the men strip down to their undergarments. After reading the story, Mary informed the others who read it also.

"Everything went just as we planned it," Almira remarked. "Why heck, they talk more about the three BUXOM BANDITS and them taking the men's clothes than about it being a stage robbery, where over seventeen thousand dollars was taken."

Mary made a mental note as to the writer's name, Abe Butler. Mary didn't know it, but their paths would cross many times in the future.

Looking once again at the front page of the paper, Mary read aloud, "'Buxom Bandits,' I like that."

A big smile on her face.

Chapter 6

By the time the train reached Denver, the wheels had been put into motion concerning Pearl's future and others like her and for the future of the Buxom Bandits.

What was originally going to be a onetime robbery to help out a friend in need, the way Mary was now looking at the big picture, that need had just increased.

"Do you have any family back home," asked Mary? "Where exactly do you call home?"

At the mention of home, Mary saw a smile come over the broken-up face of Pearl.

"A town named Concord," Pearl told her. "It's in the state of New Hampshire."

Both Mary and Pearl said together.

"I'm from Sanbornton," Mary told her.

"I don't know where that is," Pearl told her.

"It doesn't matter," said Mary. "That's where your family is from?"

"Yes," replied Pearl, still wearing the smile. "My mom, dad and my two younger sisters."

"What were you doing in San Francisco?" asked Mary.

"My daddy lost his job and we needed money. So I answered an ad in the paper for dancers and bar girls and

I got the job. All I needed to do was get out there and all living expenses would be paid. I could make fifty dollars a week and have the opportunity to make more, if I wanted to. So we scraped up the money for a train ticket."

Here, the smile left Pearl's face and tears started to flow from her blackened blue eyes.

"I was raped," Pearl said, her voice suddenly crisp and clear. "When I refused to become a prostitute, I was raped over and over by lots of different men and was beaten until I said I would," she told Mary.

"Why, those no good SOB's," Kitty said, patting her arm.

"I was told I could continue being raped and make no money, or I could do it and get paid."

Looking around at the other women, Pearl continued.

"I told them I would do it. I asked them to leave, while I got cleaned up. Once they left, I took what money I had saved to send home, snuck out the window, stole a horse, and fled to the train station where I bought a ticket for as far away as I had money for."

Mary found her train ticket and read out loud, "Omaha, Nebraska."

"What were you going to do once you reached Omaha?" asked Kitty.

Suddenly, Kitty was in a different room, in a different place in time. Years long gone of listening to her own daughter, who had run away from home with a no good boyfriend and had returned having been beaten, just as Pearl was.

Oh, but Kitty had been an angry mother and couldn't forgive her daughter for leaving. But not being able to just throw her out, had given her two hundred dollars and told her to leave and never return. She hadn't even watched her daughter leave that day, years ago. A memory now fresh in her mind.

So fresh was the memory in her mind she caught herself calling Pearl, 'April.' Embarrassed, she corrected the name to Pearl, before pushing back to let the others baby her.

As she did, Kitty caught the questioning look in Mary's eyes when they made contact. The situation at hand had brought back Kitty's own daughter and her need to talk about her. And probably, even a time to forgive.

If Mary asks, I will tell her. Kitty told herself.

"Well, Pearl," Mary spoke loudly. "You're not going to Omaha, but to Denver with us."

The whole Buxom Bandit gang nodded their heads in agreement.

Back in Denver, everything that Mary and the others had planned to do with the hold-up money had taken place.

Mary kept some cash money of which she put in a small tin with a note, which she left on Eleonore's front steps.

The note told her about the trust fund and the availability to transfer monies in the future. Further, if from time to time cash was to show up on her front steps, to spend it wisely and tell no one. Finally telling her she had a big heart and to continue helping those she could. It was signed B.B.

Kitty and Pearl formed a special bond on that trip, along with the others that lasted the rest of Kitty's life. They would all get to meet Pearl's family, see her get married, and Kitty would become godmother to Pearl's first daughter, April.

April, being the daughter Kitty had refused to let back into her life and the same daughter Kitty had learned was a prostitute, who was murdered by a drunken customer in the most lawless town in the west, Deadwood, South Dakota.

The future was looking bright for everyone, thanks to the Buxom Bandits.

All was back to normal for the five. The stage robbery had gone down in history. If you went looking through some old newspapers, you might be able to find an article or two concerning the event.

As summer drew to a close and the chilly mornings of fall set in, two things happened that rekindled the smoldering coals within the five women.

First thing to come about was a telegram from The Bank of San Francisco informing Sarah that all the money in Eleonore's trust fund had been used up.

Second, a very excited Almira informed them of a transfer of cash money from a company in Omaha to their bank here in Denver that was going to take place the following week.

"It's going to be over twenty-five thousand dollars," she told them.

"Hush up there, Almira. Why are you telling us this for?" Kitty's voice questioning. "We all agreed to never bring this subject up again. Besides, there's no need."

"I'm not so sure about that statement," Sarah's voice cut in and at the same time laid the telegram on the table where it was read by all.

Although they hadn't spoken about their stage robbery, whenever they were together it was as though each one could read the other's mind and see the desire for that excitement again

And here was the opportunity for that excitement again.

"How could Eleonore have gone through all that money so fast?" asked Leila.

"We need to go speak with Eleonore. Now," said Mary.

As the five headed to Eleonore's that crisp morning for the first time since the stage robbery, they all excitedly started to talk about what they had been holding inside, since the robbery.

By the time they reached Eleonore's, it was decided, if need be, the twenty-five thousand dollars headed for The Bank of Denver from Omaha, would never be deposited.

The surprise visit by the five caught Eleonore off guard So before either of them said a word, Eleonore threw her hands into the air and shrieked.

"I'm sorry. I lost it all."

Not waiting for any response to her outcry, she continued pacing back and forth in the room.

"Cyrus Nobles, the bank president told me he could make some investments with my trust fund money and told me he could probably double what was in it, so I told him to go ahead and invest it."

Looking from face to face, she continued.

"Cyrus informed me three days ago he had lost all of my money due to an investment he thought was going to break and make a lot of money. Instead, he told me it had gone bust and now all my money was gone."

An hour later, as the five went back to town, they knew what they were going to do. Besides, Kitty wanted to send Pearl a few dollars for her and baby April.

The next day, Almira had some information on the shipment they were going to hold up.

"Well girls, I say we need to hold up the stage as close to Omaha as possible. That way, it's in a different state, and a long way from Denver," Mary stated.

"Just what's your plan, Mary? We know nothing about Omaha! Has any of us ever been to Omaha?" asked Sarah.

"What does that matter any," Mary said. "Look, we go to Omaha, rent our horses under different names, ride out on the road the stage will travel, find a good place to hold it up. Once done, we go back to Omaha and take the next train home."

"It would be out of state," Kitty said. "Better for us."

"Omaha is such a big city, no one will even pay notice if five women were together, never mind if we separate," piped in Leila.

"I can supply us with information, plus purchase us train tickets in advance, so we don't even need to talk to anyone at the train station in Omaha. Just board the train with our tickets. Plus, I can delay giving Joe any telegrams marked for him, if it comes from Omaha and is related to a stage robbery," Almira told them.

"You girls all want to do this?" asked Mary. Her voice taking on some of the excitement all their faces showed.

"Why not!" exclaimed Kitty. "Sounds to me like it will be a new adventure and away from the homestead, so less likely to put any new light on who the Buxom Bandits really are."

"Okay then," said Mary. "Almira, as soon as we get back to town, you get the train schedules to and from Omaha.

"How long of a train ride is it to Omaha, anyways? Never mind, we'll know shortly. Let's all meet tonight at Sally's. It's already Tuesday and not much time before we need to be on our way to Omaha."

That evening they all meet at Sally's.

"You all still want to do this?" asked Mary.

The looks on each their faces told her she didn't even have to ask the question.

Almira had obtained all the train schedules. They planned on taking the late night train on Wednesday, putting them in Omaha a full day before the stage with all that money aboard was scheduled to leave.

Mary had gone through some of her and Joe's files and had found a couple of maps so they at least had some idea as to exactly where Omaha was.

"After finding the maps and looking at them, I remembered Joe saying the whole state of Nebraska was good for hauling freight because it was so flat you could make good traveling time. Which means we have to make sure we choose a good spot where we can stop the stage. Otherwise, if it senses danger and took off, it might not be possible for us to stop it."

"That isn't going to happen," Kitty said. "We get there a full day before the stage leaves which gives us plenty of time to find the right spot, even if we have to sleep out under the stars."

"Kitty is right," said Mary. "We'll find the right spot. No worries."

That Wednesday night, the five girls, with only their special traveling bags, boarded the train to Omaha.

The Buxom Bandits were ready to strike again.

Chapter 7

What played out that morning, if the playbook could have been re-written, the Buxom Bandits sure would have rewritten it.

The stage only had three on board. The driver, his partner riding shotgun, and the armed guard whose mind was set on making sure the money the stage carried made it to The Bank of Denver, at all cost.

First thing was the tree limb Mary had dragged across the road. Although positioned in an excellent place, it was also visible from some distance away giving warning to the approaching stage. So everyone was on alert.

As soon as Mary saw the stage at a distance slow down, then actually stopped, she knew this wasn't going to end well.

"They suspect something isn't right," Mary told the two who were with her. "We should call it and high-tail it outta here."

"We can't," said Sarah. "Eleonore needs the money."

"Okay, said Mary. "But let's get the other two and get out of here. I have another idea."

Making sure they weren't seen, Mary and the others rode away. Stopping on the road a short distance away, Mary laid out the new plans.

"Look girls, there are some large boulders right here. I say we hide behind them and when the stage is right here, we pop out with a couple warning shots in the air and stop it outright.

"Sarah and Kitty, you two head on up to that overlook and keep us covered, once we stop the stage."

"Okay," Kitty said. "Let's go Sarah."

"Looks like it's up to us," Mary told the others. "Are you ready?"

"Let's do it," Almira said, drawing her handgun. "I'm ready."

"I'm ready, too," Leila said.

As the stage approached the big boulder, Mary and the other two, spurred their horses out onto the road in front of it and fired a couple shots into the air and shouted for the driver to stop the stage.

The guard sitting next to the stage drive started to bring his double barrel up and into play, but a distant shot rang out and the shotgun went flying out of his hands.

Mary gave a quick glance up in the direction of the overhang where the gray puff of smoke from the rifle could still be seen. Both driver and guard threw their hands into the air at this point.

A shot rang out from inside the stage and instantly Mary's horse fell to the ground having been shot right out from under her.

Four shots rang out in quick succession and you could hear the bullets as they slammed into the stage coach.

"Urggggggggggggggggg," was heard from the inside of the stage.

The worst had happened; someone had been shot.

It was Mary's voice that cut into the air.

"That's one," Mary shouted out towards the driver and guard. "Don't make us shoot either one of you."

"Don't shoot," shouted the driver. "We have our hands in the air."

"Good, keep them there," Mary warned.

Mary got up off the ground and checked her horse, who was dead.

"Where's the strongbox?" asked Mary, shaking her pistol in his direction.

"It's inside the stage under the seat," the driver told her.

Mary indicated to Almira to check out the stage, not only for the strongbox, but to see how the person was inside.

Carefully opening the stage door, Almira looked inside. Sprawled out on the seat, but still breathing, was Matt Davis who she recognized as a person that Sheriff Joe deputized from time to time, when he need assistance.

How is it he's on this stage? Were Almira's thoughts.

Matt was also an ex-lawman who went out with Kitty from time to time.

Stepping up into the stage, Almira check Matt's wound and determined he probably wouldn't die, seeing it was only a flesh wound.

She tore off one of his shirt sleeves and made a compression bandage to stop the bleeding, at the same time telling him he'd live.

Although he said nothing, his eyes were on her and they followed her every move.

Looking under the seat she saw the strongbox. It was heavy and she struggled getting it out. Once out from under the seat, she dropped it out the door and onto the ground.

"Open the box," Mary demanded, pointing her pistol at the stage driver.

"I don't have the key," he told her.

Before Mary said another word, a shot rang out and there stood Almira over the strongbox holding a smoking gun. Looking down she saw the lock on the strongbox had been blown apart.

"Key," said Almira, holding up the smoking pistol.

Opening the strongbox, Almira went to her horse and came back with the grain sack, which she immediately started transferring the money into. When she had completed emptying the strongbox, she then made the stage driver and his partner empty their pockets and put the contents in the sack, also.

Going over to her horse and tying the sack to her saddle, Almira returned with an empty sack. She demanded they remove their outer garments, which she put in the sack telling the two they could locate them up the road apiece.

Almira then went to the horses and cut them loose. She gave them a resounding whack on their flanks and they galloped away. Once she was done, Almira re-mounted her horse and offered her hand to Mary to get aboard with her.

"Thanks, boys," they said, as the three galloped away.

Riding double sure slowed them down, getting back to Omaha.

Having to fire the shotgun from the guard's hands riding up top, and shooting up the stage and wounding Matt, it was obvious they would now know there were at least five members to the holdup gang.

"If you receive a telegram from Omaha for the sheriff and it mentions five robbers, you have to somehow change that. Joe's a smart fella and will right away have suspicions. He might not believe them, but none the less, he will have them," Mary told Almira.

"There's something else you all have to know," said Almira. "The guard who was shot was Matt Davis."

"Matt Davis!" exclaimed Kitty. "My Matt Davis?!"

"Yes, Kitty," Almira told her. "But don't worry, his wound was only a flesh wound."

It was a good thing the women had rented horses at different places and under false names because Mary's horse lay dead

She wouldn't bother going to the stable and tell them that her horse had died out on the trail, she just wouldn't go back there.

It took almost a week before a telegram showed up in Denver informing the sheriff there of the stage holdup by five suspected women. It went on to tell that Matt Davis, who was injured in the robbery, would be in on the Saturday afternoon train.

"Let me see that telegram," Mary said to Almira.

"Can any of this be changed?" Mary asked, handing the telegram back to Almira.

"Sure it can, Mary. Just have to write it over on a different note sheet," Almira told her. "What do you want the telegram to say?"

"I wish I knew what Matt Davis told them concerning the robbery," said Mary.

Not knowing what Matt, or for that matter, what the driver and his shotgun guard might have told them, Mary then said.

"Just change the number from five down to three, wait one more day then give the telegram to Joe. He ain't going to be messaging back and forth with Omaha," Mary told her.

"What do you think Joe is going to say when he gets this telegram?" Sarah asked.

"He'll probably not do much, seeing the robbery took place in Omaha. He has no authority there," Mary told them.

After their first couple of stage robberies, Mary and the others agreed it would be best if any future robberies were performed, they would travel to the surrounding states, instead of staying in Colorado.

Almira would advise them whenever a large shipment of cash was going to be on a stage bound for Denver from any of the surrounding states.

None of the girls could say which robbery changed their thoughts from needing the money for Eleonore to just robbing for the excitement. Now, they couldn't stop.

Kitty had started a scrapbook of any newspaper stories she could get her hands on concerning the Buxom Bandits. After a robbery, now Kitty would stay in the city closest to the robbery to get any articles printed on them. These articles gave them good information for doing other robberies. Plus, it was funny to read how some of the stories were blown way out of proportion.

In one article, it had all the girls stripped down and dancing and servicing all of the male passengers.

"Where in hades do they get this crap from?" asked Leila. "We're not whores."

"Stories are made up because of their embarrassment of being held up by a gang of women, who not only stole all the money, but their clothes also," Leila was told by Sarah.

"I don't like being made out to be a whore," Leila said. "Especially a cheap one."

A statement to which they all laughed.

The Buxom Bandits were surely getting a reputation, and not all bad.

Kitty started going to the city a couple of days before where they were planning a robbery. She would carefully ask around and find a family or two in need of money. So after a robbery when she would stay in the city to collect newspaper articles, she would also leave large sums of money on their front porch with a note advising them to spend it wisely and not to mention it to anyone.

But some did, and this would also be written about and they would get a new title of *Good Samaritans*.

Chapter 8

US Marshal Finch sat and listened to all that Joe had to share concerning the Buxom Bandits, and it wasn't a whole lot.

"There was only one stage robbery remotely close to here and that was at a place called Buttercup Basin. From what information I've been able to gather, this appears to be the first stage robbery attributed to the Buxom Bandits," Joe told Harry.

Joe noticed Harry looking around his office as he spoke and was a bit fidgety.

"Is there something the matter?" Joe asked Harry.

"No, nothing's the matter, just that I don't see a coffee pot anywhere," he answered. "You don't drink coffee?"

"If you want a coffee, let's go over to Sarah's bakery. Hear tell she not only has the best muffins around, but the best coffee also," Joe told him.

"Sounds good," said Harry, who was up and out of his chair before Joe finished his sentence.

Across the street, looking out Sarah's front window, when Harry and Joe stepped out through the front door and headed in Sarah's direction, was Mary.

Joe had told her all about this US Marshal Finch the agency was sending to Denver to track down the female stage robbers known as the Buxom Bandits. She was there with the other four to tell them about Finch.

"Looks like Joe and that marshal are headed in this direction," Mary said, stepping back from the window and taking her seat at the table with the others.

Sure enough, the door opened and the two stepped inside.

Joe seeing Mary, he gave her a slight nod of the head, as they entered.

"Let's take a table over there," Joe said to Harry, pointing at a table as far away as he could get from the women.

As Sarah walked over to their table, so did Mary, not letting Joe get away without an introduction. Besides, she needed to learn as much as she could about what he might know or not know, where the bandits were concerned. Heck, she was even going to ask him to supper.

"Why Joe, is this the marshal you mentioned was coming in to investigate those stage robberies?" Mary asked, knowing she had just stepped over her bounds with her husband.

Before Joe could answer, Harry was on his feet, hat in hand.

"Why yes ma'am. I'm US Marshal Harry Finch. Folks just mostly call me Harry."

"I'm Mary Day," she said, extending her hand. "I'm the sheriff's wife.

"It's a pleasure to meet you, Mary," Harry said, taking her extended hand.

"If you have a moment I'd like to introduce you to some of my friends," she said to him, ignoring *the look* from Joe.

"Some other time, Mary," Harry said.

He had caught Joe's look and wasn't going to start off on the wrong foot.

"Joe and I really need to get on with our business, plus coffee just arrived."

"Joe," Mary said turning to face him. "Invite Harry to supper tonight."

Joe's response was a slight head nod.

"Stop by in the morning, Harry. Sarah has the best coffee in all of Denver, plus she has a bacon muffin to die for."

"Ladies," she addressed her table. "Time to get on with our day."

The three got up and walked out, following Mary. Leila would return shortly, as she worked there. But for now, walked out with the others.

It was easy for Harry to read that Joe kept his work separate from his personal life with Mary. Lots of men were like that. And although Joe now had an obligation to invite him to supper, he knew Harry would refuse.

Harry was momentarily saddened by the thought Joe couldn't share his days with his wife.

One of the greatest joys he had found were the times he and Amanda would sit around over coffee and pie. She would listen and hang onto his every word, as he told her stories of all the wild adventures and close calls he had on his many assignments.

What had started as a sad thought, now put a smile on his face.

"Harry," Joe's voice echoed through the canyons of his mind, bringing him back to the here and now, but not before he noticed the dark haired woman walking out with the others.

"Sorry, Joe. I was just remembering something," said Harry.

"Mighty fine coffee, Sarah," Harry said as his cup was filled with the fresh, hot, black brew he had come to love.

"Thank you, Harry. Would you like anything else?" she asked.

"Just the bill, please," Harry replied.

"No charge, Harry. Come in anytime, and have anything you like. I hear you are here to help Joe so anything I serve is on the house," Sarah told him.

"Why thank you, Sarah. It would look like I'll be seeing you in the morning for one of your special bacon muffins and, of course, some of your delicious coffee."

"Take good care of Harry while he's here, Joe," she said, as they got up to leave.

Just as Harry was about to step through the door, he heard a low voice say.

"Her name's Kitty."

Turning to glance in the direction of the voice, he looked upon Sarah's face, just as she winked and turned away.

What had started out as another assignment just got interesting.

The rest of the day was spent gathering information. Along with wanting to speak with Matt, Harry also wanted to speak with the stage driver, the guard, and any of the passengers from the first hold-up at Buttercup Basin.

Harry couldn't help but be reminded of his lovely Amanda at the name of Buttercup Basin. Buttercups were one of her favorite wildflowers.

Not being introduced that morning, but remembering her face once again, Harry met Almira now, being introduced by Joe.

"Just call me Harry or Finch. The title 'US marshal' scares some folk off and all the time it brings out the gunslinger who wants to be remembered as gunning down a US marshal. So, Harry or Finch," he repeated.

"Deal Harry. I'm Almira," she said, extending her hand. "You can call me Almira."

Harry only wanted to see if she could supply him with any names from the robbery at Buttercup Basin, and was amazed at all she could tell him. Not only who the driver was, but when he was expected in again.

"All stage lines have several drivers with set routes they follow," she told him.

Looking at a large chalkboard on the wall with a calendar drawn on it, she pointed to that next Friday where Harry saw the names of Tommy Rhodes and Barry Simmons, followed by 'Salt Lake.'

"That's a calendar for the whole month. Along with the driver's name and his 'shotgun guard' as they have been known to be called. Also where they are coming in from. As you can see, they run the Salt Lake route which runs through Buttercup Basin," she told him.

"Wow. That's mighty impressive," Harry told her. "What do all those other numbers and marks stand for?"

"After the driver's and shotgun's name, the number is the amount of passengers so far they will be carrying. That number might change as the actual departure time arrives."

"How do you know the number of passengers aboard before they actually leave? Such as the two after Tommy's name?" he asked.

"Overland Stage Lines have what is known as 'advance purchase.' They offer a small discount for anyone purchasing a ticket in advance of the actual day of departure, so they have an idea as to how many tickets and revenue they will take in."

"That's something," Harry said.

"What's the little square in the bottom left mean?" was his next question.

Nodding toward the sheriff she told Harry, "Sheriff Joe can answer that question," she told him. "I'm not allowed."

"That little square indicates what stage will be carrying a strongbox," Joe told him.

"What I'm seeing and what I'm being told is anyone coming in to purchase a ticket or to send a telegram can see which stages will be carrying a strongbox. And can even know the driver's name and how many passengers there will be on the stage?" he asked.

The tone in Harry's voice was one of great concern and alarming.

"That board needs to come down right now. Keep your calendar with scheduling in your desk drawer, not out in the open for everyone to see," Harry told them both.

Taking a calendar from her desk drawer, Almira started to copy from the chalkboard.

"Will you make me a copy of that calendar? Do you usually make a paper copy of the schedule every month that I can have also?" Harry asked.

"No I don't, but now I will have one to file," she said. "Don't know why I didn't think of that myself."

Almira hoped she had put on a good showing. She was sure Joe didn't care much for anything that she and Harry were discussing.

"Can you get a message to the driver Tommy and Barry and make sure they plan on staying around when they come in, until Joe and I speak with them?" Harry asked.

"Sure. Will do, Harry," said Almira. "I'll send a telegram as soon as we are done here."

"We're done for now, Almira. Thank you for your time," said Harry.

"Now, I'd like to go talk with the stage guard who was shot," Harry told Joe. "What was his name again? Matt Davis?"

When Joe and Harry left, Almira started to get a sick feeling in her stomach after their meeting.

"This US Marshal Harry Finch is a smart lawman. We need to be real careful around him. We can't do another robbery while he's in town," Almira told the others.

"Did he ask or say anything else?" asked Mary.

"Only that he wanted a copy of this month's schedule. That's why I said we shouldn't do another robbery while he is here."

"I agree," said Kitty.

"I don't know about that," said Mary. "Might be a good time."

"Are you stark raving mad?" asked Leila. "Do you want to get caught?"

"Of course not," Mary said. "But think about it for a minute. If there was a stage to rob in the same place as one we have already done, we could leave some false clues around the area to throw this marshal off our trail."

"That might be a very good plan," Sarah said. "We could stage whatever we want Harry to discover."

"Ummmmm, US Marshal Harry Finch," said Kitty in a low sexy voice. "How old do you think he is?"

"Need a cold bath?" Mary asked, to which they all laughed. "Joe told me Harry was also a widower."

"Really. When did his wife pass?" Kitty asked.

"Less than a month ago," Mary told her. "She and their son died in a fire, while Harry was away on an assignment."

"How sad," Kitty said.

"I was only able to speak with Joe for a few minutes. I'm sure he knows more, but didn't have time to share with me. Anyways, I invited him to supper tonight."

"If anyone can bleed him for information, it's you Mary," Kitty said.

"Ya, that's for sure," said Sarah.

"I got a good idea," Mary said. "Kitty. Why don't you come over for supper tonight at my place?"

"Great idea, Mary," Sarah piped in. "I saw the way he looked at you, and the way you looked at him."

"The bandit and the lawman," Leila sang out. "Has a nice ring to it. Don't you all think?"

"Hey, girls. That would be a good title for a book. The bandit and the lawman or the lawman and the bandit," said Almira.

As the girls laughed and continued on with their talking, Joe and Harry needed to saddle up, if they were going to go see Matt.

Matt's place was a couple of miles north of Denver in a small community known as Pine Gap.

"Tell me about Matt," Harry said, as they made their way to Pine Gap.

The road was fairly smooth and wide enough they were able to ride side by side.

"Not much to tell," Joe said. "He's an ex-lawman in his forties who I deputize from time to time, when I need assistance. He also farms himself out as a guard sometimes at the local banks, whenever they are expecting a cash money transfer from some other bank," Joe told Harry.

"So, Matt was hired to go to Omaha and guard the shipment of money back here to the bank in Denver?"

"That's correct," Joe told him.

"What else can you tell me? Anything?" Harry asked.

"He goes out with Kitty every now and then, but according to Mary it's nothing serious," Joe told him.

"Tell me about Kitty," questioned Harry.

"Kitty? Why I think she is also in her forties. Married to some rich banker fella from Silver Springs who dropped dead a couple years back. Mary calls her the town's gossip and they have been friends since we first came to Denver," Joe told him.

Harry couldn't believe just losing his wife and son the feelings he was having for this woman Kitty, who he had just met.

Joe and Harry's meeting with Matt that day produced nothing of great value, except Harry got the feeling he was holding something back.

"You are coming to supper tonight?" Joe asked. "Mary invited ya."

"I don't normally, but I will," Harry said.

That night, Harry was surprised when he got to Joe and Mary's to find Kitty there, also.

Chapter 9

The evening spent with Joe and Mary went well and Kitty and Harry seemed to enjoy each other's company.

Harry found himself laughing like he didn't think he would ever be able to again, and the evening went by way too quickly.

Kitty was spending the night. But Harry went back to his railcar saying he would meet Joe the next morning at Sarah's for coffee, and now his second favorite thing, bacon muffins. Then he wanted to go to the scene of the stage robbery, Buttercup Basin.

Being an early riser, Harry had coffee boiling the next morning before the old cock rooster set off his wake up call.

Harry sat there in the dark, alone with his thoughts. Thoughts of his Amanda and son AJ, both he would love forever, but never see again.

These same thoughts he had every morning since their deaths, but this morning, another thought was there also. The thought of last night and Kitty.

The early morning hours went by quickly and soon it was time to meet Joe at Sarah's.

Stepping inside, Harry was surprised to not only see Joe, but Kitty as well. She looked in his direction and gave him a big smile.

Sarah was at their table pouring Harry a cup of freshly boiled coffee, just as he was taking a seat. Leila followed with a big, bacon muffin fresh out of the oven.

To Harry that morning, Kitty could have easily been Amanda. It was like Amanda to be up before him, have coffee boiling, and be her smiling, talkative self. Just as Kitty was now.

Coffee and muffin finished, Harry looked at Joe and told him it was time to get started.

As Joe and Harry got up to leave, out of the clear blue sky Kitty's voice asked, "Why don't you come to my place for supper tonight, Harry?"

Sarah and Leila gave quick glances at each other having heard Kitty's invite to Harry. After all, he was a US marshal being sent here to capture the women who have been robbing stage coaches, one of which was Kitty.

"Why, thank you Kitty, I'd love to," answered Harry.

"Good. Then I'll see you at seven. Joe will show you where I live."

Once outside, Joe told him.

"We have some hard riding to do, Harry, if you're going to make it back in time for supper with Kitty," Joe continued.

"If I were you, I'd go back in and tell Kitty to make your supper date for tomorrow night, just in case we get hung up somewhere. You might want to go on to Dawson's Landing, which was the last stop before the stage was robbed."

Taking Joe's advice, as hard as it was, Harry went back inside and changed nights with Kitty.

The trail to Buttercup Basin was a fairly nice one, other than being dry, hot, and dusty.

Joe and Harry set a fast pace. By the time they arrived in Buttercup Basin, both had to admit they had ridden enough for one day.

"Been a long time since I spent that much time in the saddle," Harry told Joe, as he stepped down off his horse and took a few moments to rub his backside.

"Now ain't you glad you told Kitty to change supper nights? We'll spend the night at that little outpost we rode by a mile back," Joe said to him.

"I was going to ask you about that. Did you ever stop there to ask if they had seen anything or anybody, especially three women?" asked Harry.

"Yes I did, Harry. This will be the second time I've been out here. If anyone at the outpost knows anything, they didn't give any information to me. But then again, folks around here keep to themselves."

"How much of this area did you check when you came out here?" Harry asked Joe.

"Not too much, Harry. That big tree limb you see there beside the trail is the one the driver said was across the road forcing him to stop the stage."

Harry reached down and manhandled the tree limb and could hardly budge it.

"They must have used a horse to drag it. I can barely budge it by myself," said Harry.

"I did the same thing, Harry, and came to the same conclusion," Joe told him.

"You told me the driver said one of the women had a travois she hauled the money box on. Did you find it or the money box?" said Harry.

"No I didn't, Harry, but I didn't look real hard either," Joe told him.

"Okay. Let's ride the trail for a short distance, then start looking for anything that resembles parts to a travois or the money box."

Harry figured they probably would have stayed on or close to the road, until they felt it safe to stop and open the money box. So he wouldn't have to venture far off the road. Knowing that place could be anywhere, Harry let instinct take charge.

About a mile or so from the robbery site, Harry found what appeared to be the travois and next to it was the money box.

"Looks like they used those big rocks to break the hinges of the box," Harry said.

"I agree," said Joe.

Harry saw something red on the ground, and picking it up found it to be a torn piece of material.

"Do you suppose that is off one of their dresses?" asked Joe.

"Yes I do," Harry said.

A continued search of the area turned up nothing else.

"Let's call it a day and head back to that outpost," said Harry. "I need a coffee and some food."

Questioning those at the outpost turned up nothing.

Next morning, as soon as Harry finished his coffee, he and Joe were back on the road to Denver.

"This was the only robbery you actually spoke to anyone about, except for Matt Davis. There have been several stage robberies over the past few months that have been attributed to the same robbers. So why haven't you spoken to more people?" asked Harry.

"Just because the monies robbed were being transferred to the bank here doesn't mean the robberies all took place around here. All the other robberies took place in surrounding states that I couldn't travel to. I don't think you will get any answers, where these women who have been called the Buxom Bandits are concerned. When we get back to my office, I'll show you something interesting and then I think you'll understand," Joe told him.

Back in Denver, sitting in Joe's office, Harry had just read the sixth story from newspapers Joe had from the surrounding states, where the other stage robberies had occurred and where the Buxom Bandits were believed to be responsible. In several stories, they were referred to as the Good Samaritans.

"They're robbing the stages to get money to give to those in need," Harry summarized.

"That was my conclusion," said Joe. "I even sent telegrams to the sheriffs in the closest cities to the stage robberies to check out and see if any of their local people all of a sudden had money to pay off old bills, but I haven't heard back from anyone yet."

With a little excitement in his voice after reading another Good Samaritan story, Harry looked up from the paper.

"What about here in Denver, Joe? Have you checked this out here?"

"Yes I have," Joe told him. "I thought I had come up with something but it turned out to be nothing."

"Let's go get a coffee and then I need to go to my railcar to change for my supper date with Kitty," Harry said. "Tomorrow, let's talk about your suspicion."

Harry started to feel a little guilty, as he readied himself for supper with Kitty. After all, Amanda and AJ had only just passed and here he was going to be in the company of another woman. A woman who made him laugh like Amanda used to.

A woman, who quite frankly had almost instantly given him feelings he thought were only for Amanda.

Harry's thoughts were also on the Buxom Bandits and what he had learned so far, which was very little. Now with what he had just been reading about them and understanding they might just be robbing the stages to help out people in need.

I'm not going to get a lot of information from anyone. Times were tough everywhere, right now, and if someone was robbing the rich to help the poor, why no one is going to give that person or persons up!

"Someone right here in Denver knows the answers," Harry said out loud.

As Harry always did, he made a mental note to go and talk with the bank president to find out who, if anybody, might have been up for a foreclosure on their homestead who suddenly came up with the money to pay the mortgage.

The next closest robbery attributed to the Buxom Bandits was in Wyoming.

Harry would have his two railcars picked up and he would go to Wyoming. But for right now, he had a supper date to attend.

"Harry, come on in," Kitty said, greeting him at the door.

Stepping inside her home, his sensors detected the aroma of boiling coffee, along with fried chicken.

Next, he caught the smell of jasmine and vanilla, two fragrances Amanda loved.

"Hope you like fried chicken, Harry," said Kitty. "I've been told mine's the best around."

"I love fried chicken, and I also love a good cup of coffee," he told her.

"Good, cause you're going to get both. Now come sit and I'll get the coffee. We can eat shortly."

Shortly was almost an hour later, as time went quickly. They sat and talked about so many different things.

It was like they both wanted to get to know everything there was to know about each other.

Personal questions were asked and answered.

To Harry, it seemed like a whole lifetime was crammed into that one hour.

Even talking about Amanda and his son didn't affect him, like he thought it would.

Harry learned there wasn't anything romantic going on between her and Matt Davis.

Kitty was proven right in Harry's book on fried chicken. By far, she made the best.

I have my own herb garden where I grow all the delicious herbs to season my chicken with," Kitty told him. "Makes all the difference, as far as flavoring goes."

"Have you ever gotten together with your friend Sarah and tried to come up with a fried chicken muffin like her bacon ones," he asked

"Why no I haven't Harry, but what a grand idea. Her bacon muffins are to die for."

After the fried chicken came a blackberry cobbler to die for. Not only did Kitty have her own herb garden she also had several blackberry bushes along with raspberry bushes, and pear, peach, and apple trees.

"Berries are in season right now. But it's a never ending battle between me and the birds," she told him.

"You don't have them covered with some netting?" asked Harry.

"I never thought of covering them up with anything. I just try to keep an eye on them as much as I can, then pick them as fast as I can before the birds get them all," and smiling, she added, "I do have a double barreled shotgun I fire into the air from time to time."

That would be exactly what Amanda would say and do, were Harry's thoughts, as Kitty told her shotgun story.

Soon the evening had to come to a close.

Walking to the door, Harry turned to once again thank her for a much enjoyed evening, as he did Kitty went up on her tippy toes and kissed him on the cheek.

"My pleasure, Harry," she said. "We can do this again when you return from Wyoming if you'd like."

"I'd like that a lot Kitty," Harry told her.

"I will only be gone for three days. When I return, I will probably go to Salt Lake, but I sure will stay long enough for another one of your meals and for an evening of your company."

"Oh, Salt Lake. We girls have shopped there before. I love Salt Lake," she told hm.

"Maybe give some thought to coming with me," he told her. "I can do my business there and you can shop. Think about it."

As Harry made his way back to his railcar, he couldn't believe what he had just suggested.

Lying in his bed later, Harry's mind played over and over again the evening he had shared with Kitty.

When he got to the part of the evening where he spoke about Amanda and AJ, he realized he had spoken about them not in grief of losing them, but in a loving memory of them. It was as if Amanda was there with him, as he spoke.

He realized they were loving memories, now. He could never have them back, so he could grieve or remember them with love.

The evening he had just had with Kitty told him his time for grieving was over. Time to get on with living and loving. He was going to be okay.

Chapter 10

Cheyenne, Wyoming was your typical western city. As Harry had expected, it gave him no new information that would help him get closer to finding the outlaw gang known as the Buxom Bandits. Although he did find a couple of newspaper stories about them in the archives of the Cheyenne Sun Chronicle.

Two different stories, but one stuck out. It was written by a reporter for the Dawson's Landing newspaper whose name was Abe Butler. It gave reference to the Buxom Bandits as the Good Samaritans, and the story he told was a lot more personal.

Abe's story was written as if he were sitting there speaking with the robbers face to face. His story told about three women who were only trying to help those families who were truly needing help.

This Abe fella had penned them as being Good Samaritans, not so much as stage robbers.

Checking the canyons of his photographic memory, Harry was sure he had seen the name before on one or two newspapers Joe had showed him in his office.

Harry was able to acquire the two newspapers and to speak with the editor, who had written the article on the stage robbery by the Buxom Bandits. In speaking with the editor, Harry learned the article by Abe Butler came over in a telegram.

When Harry asked him what he thought about the Good Samaritan angle to the stage robbers, he was surprised by the answer he received.

"Well Harry, let me say this," the editor stated.

"If you had a family and your home was about to be foreclosed, then suddenly enough money showed up on your front steps to pay off your mortgage, plus some extra to take care of your family, would you care where it came from? Would you turn the money over to the sheriff? What would you do, Harry?" he asked.

"Now, you can go talk to the bank president if you want to blow off some time. But I can tell you right now, you won't find out anything. Banks are hurting also, and if someone can pay their debts, well, they don't care where the money comes from."

"I have a feeling you know a lot more than what you're telling me. I can respect a man's decision for not wanting to say anything, but I'm a lawman and I have been assigned a job to do. I can't let something this personal get in the way of doing my job," Harry told him.

"The money robbed belonged to other people, it's not theirs to take and give out to whoever they deem needy, regardless of what the circumstances might be," Harry concluded.

"Well Harry, you have your job cut out for you," he was told. "Look around at the empty homesteads. If you had the money to save just one of them, would you and not care where the money came from?"

Harry had heard all he needed to from the editor.

He would have to go speak with the bank president, no matter how or what he was feeling now.

Amanda had shown Harry how compassionate one human being could be towards another. She showed him how compassionate Jesus was to others, even when faced with his own death.

In speaking with the bank's president, Harry got just the answers he had expected, which had amounted to nothing.

Looking around at all the activity going on, Harry saw a town getting along just fine. But at what cost and whose money?

After Harry left the bank, his questions to others were met with cold shoulders. He felt the unwelcoming attitude of the people he spoke with. Knowing he wasn't going to get any more cooperation from anyone, Harry went back to the train station to wait to be picked up for his return to Denver.

Harry knew if, in fact, this Abe Butler had actually met the Buxom Bandits and there was truth to what he had written about them being looked upon as Good Samaritans, he was going to have a very hard time finding out who they were, other than catching them in the act or having them turn themselves in.

The constant swaying of his railcar along with the constant clickity clat, clickity clat brought on by where the rails were joined together, soon had Harry mesmerized.

Harry was hoping that once he met Abe, he would be able to get enough information from him to be able to make an arrest. Harry was sure Abe had met them face to face and knew who they were. Harry was skeptical he would get any information from him at all, even if threatened with prison time.

Harry figured that, other than a small piece of red material, he had nothing else. Whenever Harry passed through a town with dancing girls and prostitutes, he would go looking for a red dress that was missing a torn off piece of material.

Harry knew his best bet was to speak with Abe and when he returned to Denver, he would have Almira contact Abe and have him come to Denver.

The aroma of boiling coffee brought Harry back from his trance.

"I wonder what Kitty is doing right about now," Harry asked himself.

If Harry only knew what Kitty was really up to, he would die inside.

She, Mary, and Almira were standing in the middle of the trail somewhere in Logan County, Kansas with their firearms pointed at the stage driver and his shotgun guard demanding they toss down the strongbox the stage was carrying.

In that strongbox coming from Dodge City to destination The Bank of Denver, was close to twenty thousand dollars

The Buxom Bandit's weren't going to pull off a robbery while the US marshal was in the city. But upon hearing the amount the stage would be carrying, they couldn't resist.

The Bandits weren't going to waste any time. So as soon as the strongbox hit the ground, so did all three with Mary running to the stage, opening the door, and telling everyone inside to get out.

Two shots rang out. Mary looked in their direction to see Almira stuffing money from the strongbox into a grain sack. This was Mary's cue to have the passengers empty their pockets and disrobe, along with the driver and shotgun guard.

"Thank you, my honey bees," said Almira, getting back on her horse and moving over to cut the team loose.

"Find the team and you find your clothes," Kitty said, putting heels to flanks and speeding out of there in a big cloud of dust.

The girls would need to ride hard to the stage hub in Rank, Colorado, where they would catch a stage to Colorado Springs, then a train to Denver.

Depending on how Harry was making out, they were in hopes of making it back to Denver before him. If they didn't, then it would just go down as their monthly girl's trip into the city.

Almira could post their tickets for anyplace she wanted. After all, she was the ticket agent in Denver. In the past, she had done this very thing in order to not leave a paper trail if a lawman came around snooping.

The girls laughed and joked for a good part of the trip back to Denver. In between storytelling, Mary looked over to Kitty and asked.

"What's the latest going ons with the marshal?"

Kitty's face lit up some at the mention of Harry.

"Nothing," she answered. "I just made him some fried chicken, pie, and coffee that's all. We sat around and talked about a thousand different subjects. He even told me about his dead wife and son."

"Did he mention why he was here in Denver?" asked Mary.

"No he didn't. But he did say he was here working on a case with the sheriff, so we all know what that case is. He's looking for us," Kitty said laughing. "I'm entertaining the US marshal sent here to capture me along with all of you, and Mary is married to the sheriff who's also looking to capture us, and we just pulled off another stage robbery right under both of their noses."

"All of this is funny, and I could sit here laughing along with you all, but I can't," said Mary. "Although there are a lot of people that cheer us on, there are those who want to see us behind bars. There are those who won't stop looking till we are. You all understand that, right?"

"Mary, we all knew what we were getting into from the get-go. You made that perfectly clear to us all and we made our choice," Almira said in her no nonsense voice.

"Listen Mary, the stage we just robbed, and the money in this sack, I'm looking at it as our last big hurrah. We all knew the stakes involved, and we made our choice like Kitty said.

"This stage robbery, I think we all know why we did it at this time. We don't need to come out and say it," Sarah said, although her words were directed to Mary, they were intended for them all.

"Hopefully we make it back before Harry does, and if we do, Almira, I want you to once again contact Abe and set up a meeting with him. Let's give him another story to write. Set the meeting up like you have in the past. He can be trusted to follow your directions," Mary told her.

"What are your intentions?" asked Leila.

"Well," said Mary. "I want you all to do some deep down thinking over the next day or two as to the Buxom Bandits giving themselves up or fading into the sunset."

"What are you saying Mary?" Leila asked. "We give ourselves up!"

"I'm saying to think about it, that's all. If we gave ourselves up now, we might get some leniency from a judge. If not, remember there is still a price on our heads that will bring out every bounty hunter and young whippersnapper set on bringing in the notorious stage robbers, the Buxom Bandits."

"You girls can do what you want. But I'm not giving myself up. I'll take my chances," Almira spoke up.

"Me too," voiced the others.

After which, they all turned to face Mary, their faces questioning.

"Of course, I'm with you all," said Mary. "I just had to know where you all stood."

"Well, don't question our loyalty again. If you do, no more fried chicken stuffed muffins for you," threatened Sarah.

Turning to Kitty, Sarah continued.

"What a delicious idea that was of Harry's. They are my number one selling item."

"Well, ya, you practically beat me with a stick to get the chicken to frying. so you could make some to try."

"Wow! I have a great idea," Leila said excitedly. "We could do specials like, beef stuffed muffins or venison stuffed or bear, we get the guys to bring us in a deer, bear or turkeys and that becomes our special till it's gone."

"What about adding a gravy topping?" asked Kitty.

And just like that, the subject matter changed. So the remainder of their stagecoach robbery adventure turned to one of cooking.

Gone were any concerns about being caught or turning themselves in, or being captured by law or bounty hunter.

If a stranger was riding with them listening to their conversation, they never would have guessed these five laughing ladies had just held up a stage at gunpoint, took all its money, made everyone strip down to their undergarments, and rode off with them. No one would ever give a thought of them being the Buxom Bandits.

Chapter 11

Mary and the girls arrived back in Denver before Harry returned. As for Joe, he had been so busy with work, he hardly knew she was gone.

There had been a fire over at old man Simpson's place. And for a couple of cowboys who wanted to shoot up the town, he had locked away in the jail house. But the most disturbing was the young whore who lay near death at Eleonore's.

She had been severely beaten by a customer who told Sheriff Joe she had stolen money from his pants pocket.

In most cases in the old west, a prostitute was a lesser figure than a farm animal. The dirt on the soles of your boots. No one paid much attention to a beaten, or a dead whore for that matter. Except, this was Denver and Joe Day was the sheriff.

Joe had watched his wife closely over the years, and, believe it or not, had learned a few things from Mary.

Joe didn't always show it, but inside he was a very compassionate guy. Hadn't always been one, but watching his wife and her friends with the orphaned children, plus the couple of times they brought a beaten, bloodied whore to Eleonore's place had shown him something he hadn't grown up with. The compassion shown from one person for another.

Something changed inside Joe that evening he picked up this beaten, near death young woman. He carried her to the only person he knew was going to help her, Eleonore.

As Joe laid her on the bed Eleonore pointed him to, he noticed some of her blood had stained his shirt and his hand. For reasons unknown to him, Joe closed his eyes and willed his own life's blood to replace that which this young girl had lost.

This experience he shared with his wife, when they were sitting on the porch swing, having an after supper coffee and looking at the billions of twinkling stars that carpeted the heavens. Then, he never brought it up again.

There would be times in their lives, after that experience, where Mary would be on the verge of leaving Joe. But because he had shared this one deep emotional experience with her, he had shown her his heart. That would overcome any thoughts of her leaving.

After hearing Joe's story, Mary told the others she was going to go to Eleonore's place. They should bring their bags home and then meet her there.

"Okay Mary, we'll meet you shortly. Let's go girls," Sarah told the others.

"Joe, would you walk with me to Eleonore's?" asked Mary.

"Sure," he answered. "But first, I need to stop at the office."

Unlocking the office and stepping inside, Joe told her he would be back in a few minutes. He then opened the door to the jailhouse and disappeared inside.

Mary walked over to his desk and sat in his chair. It was then she saw the newspapers. Opening up one of them, Mary saw the circled story. It was a story about the Buxom Bandits, written by Abe Butler.

Looking at some of the other papers, she saw all the stories concerning the Buxom Bandits had been circled. Checking them all, she realized there was a paper from every city where they had robbed a stage.

All of the other stories were written by Abe Butler, too, and she remembered every one.

The excitement they all showed as they sat with him and answered his questions. All the while dressed up in their whore dresses and sportin' lots of makeup.

"So Joe did know about the stage robberies," Mary whispered out loud.

Mary figured the papers were left out because Joe had shown them to Harry. She was sure Harry would have looked at who wrote the stories and discovered they were all written by the same person.

The jail house door opened and Joe walked back into the office.

"Is everything okay, Joe?" asked Mary.

"All is good. I have two cowboys locked up and wanted to see if they needed to use the outhouse," said Joe.

"Who are these Buxom Bandits?" asked Mary. "Are they the reason Harry is here?"

"Yes, Mary. These stage robbers are the reason Harry is here," Joe told her.

"There's three of them, according to one of the stories," Mary stated.

"That's what's written," said Joe. "But Harry and I believe the number is probably five. We'll know for sure in the next few days."

"How will you know that?" Mary questioned.

She was hoping Joe would continue talking.

Careful Mary, she told herself, knowing Joe had already told her more than he had ever about his work.

"I thought Almira would have told you. Harry had her contact the stage line to find out when the driver of the stage that was robbed coming out from Omaha would be through here again. He wants to talk with him."

Joe picked up one of the newspapers and pointed to the circled story.

"This is the story that was written about the stage robbery which took place with that Omaha stage," Joe told her. "Read the story."

"The story says the stage was held up by three women," Mary told him. "It doesn't say anything about five women."

"No it doesn't, but where it tells about the guard riding shotgun starting to pull up his gun, then out of nowhere a shot rang out, which blew the shotgun out of his hands. Didn't say, one of the three shot the shotgun from his hands, but a shot out of nowhere did."

"I see where one would think there was another person maybe hiding in the bush," Mary said.

"That's right. And so did the guard inside the stage that was shot. The driver said there were four shots fired at the stage when he had fired from inside killing one of the bandit's horse," Joe continued.

Without finishing his thoughts, Joe took the newspaper from Mary's hand, placed it with the others, and told her it was time to go home.

So, this marshal believes there to be five bandits, does he? Was Mary's thought as she and Joe made their way home.

Hindsight is great. Now with this information, Mary wished they wouldn't have pulled off this last stage robbery. Mary figured they still had the advantage. Knowing what Harry knew could only benefit them.

Once they meet with Abe and give him a new story to write, then lay low for a while, she was in hopes Harry would leave, Joe would just go back to being the sheriff, and the Buxom Bandits would be a thing of the past, having ridden off into the wild, blue yonder, never to be seen or heard from again.

The next morning, Joe went to his office and Mary headed over to Sarah's, where she knew the others would be. Twenty minutes later, she had told them everything she had learned the night before from Joe.

Harry was due on the ten o'clock train, but the stage wouldn't be in until five.

"If Harry thinks there were five women involved in the stage robberies, do you think he would suspect us?" asked Leila.

"Just because he suspects there are five, there was no mention that the two he speaks about have to be women. They could be men for all he knows," Mary told them.

"I need to be going to the office," said Almira. "Are we going to meet at Mel's for lunch?" she asked.

"Kitty, why don't you meet the train that Harry will be arriving on, and invite him to have lunch with us," Mary told her.

"I'll do that," Kitty answered.

Kitty was sitting in the train depot office talking to Almira, as she waited for the train Harry would be on, when the telegraph key started with its dots and dashes. Almira hastily wrote down the incoming message for Sheriff Joe.

The message was from Sheriff Tommy Tucker from Dodge City, Kansas, advising the sheriff of the stage robbery by the then known Buxom Bandits.

The message went on to say one of the passengers might have recognized one of the holdup women.

"Holy crap!" exclaimed Almira, once she had finished jotting down the message.

"What is it?" Kitty asked at Almira's outburst.

"Someone thinks they know who one of the women stage robbers is," replied Almira, just as the train whistle sounded.

"Go ahead and meet Harry and bring him to Mel's as planned. You do realize, Kitty, you and Harry will never happen," Almira told her.

With that, she was gone, leaving Kitty standing there with the understanding that Almira was right.

"Harry and I will never happen," she said out loud.

Harry had mentioned to her in their conversation he had a private railcar, but what he showed her now was nothing she had imagined.

The walls inside the car were hand rubbed Mahogany wood. All the furnishings were a plush velvet material of a dark cranberry color. The aroma was of boiling coffee.

It had everything a house would have.

It's a nice surprise you meeting me," Harry told her.

He remembered Amanda always met him at the station, when he returned from an assignment.

A smile crossed his face.

"Penny for your thoughts," Kitty's voice sounded. "Happy thoughts, by the smile on your face."

"Just remembering a different place in time and a different woman," Harry said in a soft voice.

"Amanda," Kitty whispered, at the same time placing her hand on his arm.

Without realizing what he was doing, Harry bent down and placed a soft kiss on Kitty's lips. Almost at once after having done this, Harry backed away.

Harry saw the questioning look on Kitty's face, followed by her gentle touch on his arm.

"It's okay, Harry. I felt the same feelings of betrayal when I was kissed the first time, after losing my husband. I think it's only normal to feel like that," she whispered.

"You are so much like her that it just seemed natural," said Harry.

"Don't look at this as you trying to replace Amanda, or even think I would want to. One person can't replace another Harry, especially if the person was a spouse."

"I can hear Amanda saying those exact words," said Harry. "Thank you."

"Don't mention it, big fella," she now jokingly told him. "Now let's get on over to Mel's, I'm starving!"

Kitty decided right then and there whatever happens between them happens. She wasn't going to let the words of someone else deter her. Something was happening between her and Harry and she was going to let it play out.

I'll face the music when and if that time comes. These were her thoughts, as they walked to Mel's.

"Did you get any new information about the Buxom Bandits, Harry?" Mary questioned, as they sat around after their meal.

Harry shot Joe a questioning look.

"Joe didn't tell me, Harry," Mary said, picking up on his look in Joe's direction.

"I was in his office and saw some newspaper stories on them. Must be exciting to be going here and there tracking down the bad guys," she continued.

"There are times it's exciting. But most of the time you're on horseback, in the rain or cold, or it's so dang hot you sweat until your clothes are soaking wet. The real excitement comes when you get so darn close to capturing them, you can taste it. That's when it starts to get exciting," he told her.

"So, Harry, are you close on the trail of these Buxom Bandits? Do you have any idea who they are?" asked Mary.

"No, I don't. But I'm pretty sure I know who does," he told her.

Only years of training and knowing what to look for, and when it was needed, to pick up the secretive look between Mary and Kitty. He wasn't even looking for it, or much less expecting one, but there it was. It's at times like these in conversation where those years of experience start to pay off.

Harry could tell he was being drilled for information concerning the women stage robbers and he was going to keep the conversation going as long as he could. What made the conversation interesting was who was doing the drilling.

Gut feeling told Harry something was going on here. So he decided to bait the hook a little to see what transpires.

If I'm on the right track, I know what the next question will be and caution them not to breathe a word to anyone.

"So tell us, Harry, who do you suspect these stage robbing women to be?" asked Kitty, taking Harry's bait.

"I'll know more after I talk with this reporter, Abe Butler. But I'm pretty sure the woman who runs the orphanage, Eleonore, is involved or for sure knows who is. You can't breathe a word of that to anyone. Do you ladies understand that?"

Now to wait for their next move.

Harry was feeling down knowing Kitty was probably involved somehow, but he didn't let his suspicions be known to anyone.

"Almira, would you or could we go to the station? I meant to have you give me a schedule and a ticket to Omaha for tomorrow. Plus, it's time for the stage to arrive. I want to catch the driver and ask him a few questions."

Almira went with Harry and gave him the schedule and a ticket for Omaha, then Harry went to his railcar to wait for the stage.

After questioning the stage driver, Harry was sure there were at least five bandits involved in his stage robbery and was sure he would be able to find the place where the driver said the robbery took place.

Harry had a terrible night's sleep. Several times during the night he was awakened by being chased by five women on horseback. When they started to fire at him, he woke. There was nothing about them he recognized. Like he had been told, they wore a lot of makeup, but he did see a torn, red dress.

Chapter 12

"What do we do now, girls? We just heard Harry say he thinks Eleonore is involved in the stage robberies and a part of the Buxom Bandits," Mary said.

This is not the way any of them thought the end of the Buxom Bandits would come about. Even possibly having to turn themselves in to protect their friend.

"Eleonore will have plenty of alibis. She has nothing to worry about," Sarah told them.

"Of course she will, dummy," said Mary. "She's not one of the bandits, so she knows nothing."

The girls had left and were in the train depot office where Almira worked, so she could be there in case word of their latest stage robbery came across the telegraph.

"Almira, time to draw up those fake tickets and take the real ones off the docket, so no one can trace our travels," Mary told her.

"Okay, that's done. Here are some ticket stubs we can show for our trip to San Francisco, if we need to," Almira said, handing each of them a stub.

"Abe is on his way here, also," Almira told them.

"When will he arrive?" Mary asked.

"You want to share with us exactly what's on your mind? Because it seems like you have got something else on your mind other than just giving Abe a story," asked Sarah.

"You all heard Harry, tonight. He thinks Eleonore has something to do with the bandits and he is going to try to prove that, but we can't let that happen. It would ruin her and the orphanage," Mary told them.

"What would you suggest we do now? You're right, we can't let that happen," asked Sarah.

"No we can't and we won't. We have to come up with a story to give Abe that will somehow satisfy Harry that the bandits are not here and that he needs to be looking somewhere else for them," Mary told them.

"Joe told me the stage robberies which have occurred, even though in different states, still fell within Harry's jurisdiction. Maybe we need to find out where his jurisdiction ends and do a robbery there," Mary suggested.

"Do you think that would really work? If you do, I can probably get the information from Harry, but what's the point?" asked Kitty.

"If the bandits are no longer in his area, but somewhere else, why would he stay here? The case would go to someone else and he would be taken off it," Mary questioned.

Turning to Almira, Mary asks,

"Is there any way to get a barren money stage's schedule? Let's say for Saint Louis. No, let's say Washington D.C.?"

"Are you nuts?" asked Sarah.

"I guess I am. Let's just wait until we know where Harry's jurisdiction is. But we have to know that right away before we meet with Abe. Kitty, do you think you can get that information from Harry before he leaves in the morning?" answered Mary.

"I think you should see if Joe can. This Harry is smart. We don't want him to train his sights on any of us. Plus, it's lawman to lawman conversation," Kitty answered back.

"I'll talk to Joe tonight," said Mary. "He meets with Harry every morning at your place, Sarah. Hopefully, he can find out then. Once we know his jurisdiction, then we can plan a stage robbery outside of it."

"What should I do with this telegram for Joe from Sheriff Tucker of Dodge City?" asked Almira. "Someone on the stage said he recognized one of us."

"No one on that stage recognized any of us. For crying out loud, if Matt didn't recognize you, some cowboy on a stage in Dodge City sure didn't either. Hold off on giving that to Joe, right now. He plans to go to Omaha, let him go. He'll be gone a few days so we have some time to plan our next move," said Mary.

"What about Abe?" was Almira's next question.

"It's too late to stop him now. So once he gets to town, if we still don't know what we are going to do, I'll meet with him by myself. I can deliver him a telegram from the bandits, which you can write up, Almira, on telegram paper to make it look legit," said Mary.

"I don't know about you all, but this girl needs some beauty sleep," Kitty remarked, to the laughter of all. "Let's call it a day."

Almira shut down everything and everyone went home.

Mary was going to talk with Joe. She made him something special, so they could sit and talk over coffee on the porch swing. She had noticed the last few times that she and Joe had some meaningful conversation, that it was on the porch swing over coffee and dessert. She enjoyed those times.

For some reason, unbeknownst to her, Joe became a different person at those times and she looked forward to them. It was on that old swing she even heard him belly laugh, a couple of times.

Tonight, sitting there with Joe, she felt he was deep in thought. He wasn't his usual self, when they sat out there together.

It had been some time since Mary had seen this side of him again, and knew he was trying to put something into words to tell her. She knew at these times, she had to be the one to open the conversation.

"Penny for your thoughts, Joe?" she asked, placing her hand on his shoulder.

Mary knew as soon as she asked the question, there would be no beating around the bush with Joe. He was still a man of few words. And this time was no different.

"I want to be a US marshal," he told her.

"You what! Did I just hear you say you wanted to be a US marshal?" she exclaimed.

Mary knew what she had heard, and recognized the tone of voice she had heard it in. The same tone Joe had used when he had told her he wanted to become the sheriff of Denver.

She knew in his mind he was already a US marshal and once that came about, there would be no telling him different. If Joe wanted to be a US marshal, Joe would become a US marshal.

Blindsided by this, Mary was agape for a few seconds with the thought of who she was secretly, and who he wanted to be in real life.

Mary captured her thoughts. There were hundreds circling around inside her head and she needed to concentrate on getting the information she needed at present. Suddenly, she had her answers.

"Will that mean we have to move? Don't marshals have set territories they are responsible for? Isn't Denver Harry's territory?" she asked.

Then in a stern voice, she told him, "I'm not moving, Joe."

"US marshals do have territories they oversee. And yes, this is Harry's territory. But he is in the Midwest. He doesn't patrol the southwest, such as Arizona, New Mexico, Texas, and Oklahoma."

There it is. Harry's territory. We can do a stage robbery in one of those states, were Mary's thoughts. *This is going to get really messy,* was another.

"Have you spoken to Harry concerning this matter?" Mary asked, regaining her composure.

"Not yet," Joe told her. "I figure I'd wait till this case gets closed."

An idea popped into Mary's head. She would give it more thought to this idea during the night, so she would have clarity on it in the morning. Mary knew for her that it would pretty much be a sleepless night. But by morning, she had worked up a good plan providing train schedules that matched.

The more Mary thought about Joe becoming a US marshal, the more even the thought of moving had some new potential.

Racing to meet the girls the next morning, Mary couldn't wait to tell them everything Joe had told her. Plus, all the new thoughts she had during her sleepless night.

When Joe and Harry walked into Sarah's the next morning, Mary and the girls were walking out. They were headed to the station, so Almira could start looking up schedules and telegraphing different cities for information on possible gold and money shipments. Kitty stayed behind a few minutes to talk with Harry.

It was decided, if scheduling allowed, Almira would give the telegram from Sheriff Tucker of Dodge City to Harry, but to take away the mention of recognition by one of the passengers.

Hopefully, Harry would want his trip changed to go to Dodge City directly from Omaha, This would be the time the bandits needed to pull off another stage robbery, outside of Harry's jurisdiction, setting in motion all they had discussed previously.

Before Harry left, he asked Kitty if she wanted to join him.

"I wish I could Harry, but the girls and I plan on going back east to see Pearl and my goddaughter April, plus do some shopping," she answered.

Telling Harry this, along with Almira issuing them tickets, set in motion their alibi.

Mary and Almira had looked at several options. They had to pull off a robbery during the time Harry would be gone, if he chose to go to Dodge City after Omaha. Right now, their plan was to get on the next train, right after Harry left.

Mary would tell Joe they were all going back east with Kitty to see Pearl and April and shop. When in reality, they would go to Las Vegas, New Mexico where they would hold up the stage bound for Albuquerque.

Almira couldn't tell them if there was much money on board, but the stage did carry a money box. Nonetheless, the robbery would seal their presence in New Mexico and out of Harry's jurisdiction.

Everything was going just like a picture puzzle. Pieces were falling into place. When Harry was given the telegram from Sheriff Tucker from Dodge City and planned on going there after Omaha, well, that was the last piece of the puzzle, as far as the girls were concerned. Except for Abe, who they would leave a message for, to take a room at the hotel and wait for further correspondence.

Harry sat in his railcar listening to the ever constant rumbling of the steel wheels going over rail seams and felt the familiar rocking of his railcar. His eyes, although gazing out the window at the passing landscape, saw nothing. Harry was deep in thought.

The herds of Buffalo roaming the plains went unnoticed. So did the vultures picking at some dead animal they had discovered.

Harry's sensors weren't even picking up the aroma of the fresh coffee he had boiling on the stove. This was the typical Harry, as he sifted through all the information he had gathered so far concerning the Buxom Bandits.

His conclusion so far kept repeating in his head, and one that troubled him. *Eleonore, Kitty, Mary, Sarah, Leila, and Almira all have to be involved,* he thought.

Harry was hoping with this new information about another robbery in Dodge City, he would be able to verify his claim or not as to who the Buxom Bandits are.

A rail accident at North Platte set him back several hours. By the time he did reach Omaha, it was night fall and would be too dark to ride out to the spot where the stage robbery had taken place.

His railcar unhitched, Harry went and found the sheriff and introduced himself. Then invited the sheriff to go and eat with him.

Sheriff Rodney Banks was a good guy. In his early forties, he was a solid rock. Treated everyone with respect, while demanding respect in return. Harry got along good with Sheriff Banks, but learned nothing new.

Sheriff Banks told Harry he would go with him to the actual site of the hold up, but he had already taken several men, scoured the whole area, and found nothing. Harry still wanted to see and walk the site of the hold up.

When he did this, he was somehow reliving the robbery, as it happened. This was the only robbery where shots were fired and someone was injured. He was hoping to locate some clue that was overlooked by Sheriff Banks.

Sitting on Duke in the middle of the road where it was believed to be the spot where the stage was stopped, Harry scanned the area.

It was here that the stage guard had his shotgun blown out of his hands, and as Harry looked over the area he saw the imaginary puff of smoke from a rifle blast. Stepping down off Duke, he walked over to that area.

Sheriff Banks watched as Harry bend down and picked something up from the ground. When he returned, Harry handed him a spent Winchester Model 1873 cartridge.

"That casing proves there was someone else hiding out besides the three robbers," said Harry. "They missed picking that one up."

"Let's be heading back," said Harry. "I need to catch the five o'clock train to Dodge City."

Harry thanked Sheriff Banks for his help.

Once again Harry sat listening to the familiar sounds of the rail car, while feeling the slight swaying motion.

Harry was sitting and waiting for the coffee to boil. He was looking at the red piece of material and the spent cartridge from one of the most popular rifles, the Winchester Model 1873, which there had to be thousands out there.

Harry had been to three locations and had turned up two physical clues. He knew he would have to go to the other robbery sites.

As Harry's railcar headed west, the Buxom Bandits sat on their leased horses in the middle of the road. They were waiting for the stage from Albuquerque to pull around the bend, where they had dragged a large tree limb across the road.

If everything went as planned, they would be back in Denver a full day before Harry returned.

Everything did go off as planned, but the bandits did get quite a surprise. Without being told, the driver and the guard riding shotgun started to take off their clothes without being ordered to. This was a sign the Buxom Bandits were known in New Mexico.

There was only five thousand dollars in the strongbox, but at least it would seal their presence there. Not knowing any organization to give the money to, they put it in a small sack with a note and left it on the altar of a church. Now all they need to do was get back home and finish setting their alibis.

Almira had contacted Abe and he should be at the hotel in Denver, waiting for their contact.

Denver looked different to Mary, as she gazed around the streets from the train depot.

She and the other Buxom Bandits had just arrived back from New Mexico.

If the Padre of that little church did as the note said, well, his little church and its members were five-thousand dollars richer thanks to the *Good Samaritans*.

Aka: The Buxom Bandits.

Epilogue

It's said, if you make plans, something always goes wrong. This was not the case with the Buxom Bandits. Oh no, just the opposite.

Everything Mary had hoped for concerning the Buxom Bandits came true.

Waiting for Harry's return, Mary met with Abe, the reporter, on behalf of the Buxom Bandits. She told him the story hasn't ended yet. She promised him when it did, she would contact him again in the next couple of days, all of which he agreed to.

Harry meet with Sheriff Tommy Tucker of Dodge City, the place of the last stage robbery. A visit to the site of the robbery turned up nothing.

The witness who said he recognized one of the holdup women, well he turned out to be a drunkard and the woman he said he knew was a local prostitute by the name of Teddy Bear, simply because she reminded him of a very large, huggable, teddy bear, who you could tell had never been on a horse in her life. Nor wanted to.

Almira told Harry that Abe was at the hotel. He went to talk with him, taking Joe along.

Right from the start, Harry could see Abe had been warned against giving him any real, helpful information where the Buxom Bandits were concerned.

Harry was once again at a standstill. He was almost certain he knew who the bandits were, but didn't have anything to really prove that fact.

That night, after having dinner with Kitty, she told him that while he was gone, she and the girls had gone back east to visit Pearl and April. And that Kitty had decided to move back east to be close to them and help raise her new goddaughter.

Also that night, just before Harry went to sleep, his telegraph key went off advising him of the new robbery which took place in New Mexico, believed to have been done by the Buxom Bandits.

Suddenly, Harry was wide awake. If that was true and was proven, it would mean he will be pulled off the case. Then, it would fall under the Southwest territory, which he wasn't responsible for, and be handed off to US Marshal Dawson Patterson. Harry knew Dawson very well and had wired him a couple of times in regards to this case.

Harry knew that by tomorrow night, he would either still be on the case or be headed for his new home on Ogallala. This would be the only case to date he didn't close. And this fact he couldn't fathom at this time.

"I know who they are," Harry spoke out loud to the telegraph key.

Harry had never faced not winning and he was having a hard time with the thought of it.

"I'm jumping to conclusions here. I need to wait and hear for certain," Harry said.

Harry almost didn't hear the knock on his door, it was so quiet. Answering it, Harry welcomed Joe inside, wondering why he was here. Joe had never been inside Harry's railcar in all the time he was here.

"Joe, what a surprise," Harry said, offering Joe his hand. "What can I do for you?"

Although it was exciting for Harry to hear Joe talk about wanting to be a US marshal, he also knew it wasn't the job for him. Harry set about trying to show him that by asking him a very tough question.

"Joe, you seem to be content with your job as sheriff here in Denver. You have a loving wife, a nice home, you're home every night, and some folks to call 'friends.' All this is what every one of us strives for. You have that now, why do you want to change all of that?" Harry asked.

"Don't answer that now. Think on it. Here's another one I want you to think on. What if you discovered that the Buxom Bandits were someone you knew? Could you arrest them? What about having to be away from home for an unknown length of time? Could you and your wife handle that?" Harry said.

Harry could have gone on, but the look on Joe's face told him he didn't have to say anything more.

As much as Joe might have wanted to be a US marshal, the reality was he knew he couldn't do the job as would be needed.

So he stayed in Denver and won the next year's election. Even though he wasn't able to capture the Buxom Bandits, Denver was never plagued by them again.

The Buxom Bandits through Abe's stories would, for the rest of their existence, be known as the Good Samaritan Stage Robbers. They would go on performing stage robberies throughout the country, going into the different jurisdictions of the US marshals and never robbing in the same jurisdiction twice in a row.

Through Eleonore's organization, she unknowingly would supply Mary and the Good Samaritans information on other orphanages and organizations needing financial help. They would find a grain sack on their doorsteps, stuffed with money and a note. And they always included a small sum of money be left on a church's altar with a note to use as needed for local families in need.

There would be countless stories written up about them and they were credited with saving the lives of many a homesteader.

The Good Samaritans would go down in the books as real live folk heroes, thanks to Abe Butler's stories and his imagination for telling a good story.

After every stage robbery, he would get a telegram telling him where to meet. Once in a room, there would be a chair with a curtain divider. Someone on the other side would relay the hold up to him. From that, he would write a story. In Abe's stories it was considered an honor to be robbed by the Good Samaritans.

Passengers would automatically strip off their outer garments without being ordered to, laughing while they did. Then empty their pockets of their personal possessions.

There was never a shot fired after the robbery when Matt Davis was shot.

Abe would be threatened with jail time, if he didn't cooperate with the US Marshals Office and divulge his source for his stories, but he never served any. Even on his death bed, his lips stayed sealed. If he knew their identity, he took it to the grave with him.

And then there was US Marshal Harry Finch.

As was true with many lawmen, and even so today, there is always that one case you work on and never solve. This was true with Harry's father in the case involving the Engraver, and would be true in Harry's case involving the Buxom Bandits.

Although Harry was pretty sure he knew who the Buxom Bandits were, he was pulled off the case before he was ready to make an arrest.

Several different marshals after him tried to capture them, but without success. The Buxom Bandits eventually dropped out of sight, never to be apprehended.

Kitty, who he had met while on that assignment and could have fallen in love with, moved back east to be with her sort of adopted daughter and helped raise her goddaughter.

Harry had a trophy case of items he had collected from all the cases he had been assigned to and solved.

In the case of the Buxom Bandits, Harry had a red piece of material. He was certain it came from one of the Buxom Bandits' dresses. He carried it around with him at all times, never failing to check out any woman he saw wearing a red dress.

In the future, whenever Harry was on assignment and in Denver, he always spent some time with Sheriff Joe and his wife Mary.

Harry never did reveal to Joe his suspicions about Mary and her friends. But what he was almost certain of was their relationship to the Buxom Bandits.

Harry did move to Ogallala, never remarried, and went on to solve many other cases before he retired.